HEAR YE! HEAR YE!
HIS MAJESTY, THE KING,
WISHES TO ANNOUNCE
THE WHIRLWIND WEDDING
OF HIS YOUNGEST,
PRINCESS SERENA,
TO LOYAL ROYAL BODYGUARD
GABRIEL MORGAN

LET IT BE KNOWN that **Serena** (long the rebellious daughter—and bane of every royal bodyguard she gave the slip!) married her protector in Ye Olde Wedding Chapel in Las Vegas, U.S.A. (Not the queen's first choice... if she were given a choice, that is!)

LET IT ALSO BE KNOWN that **Gabriel Morgan**, royal defender extraordinaire and long a favorite of the king's (though a man of many secrets) is the newest Wyndham son.

All of Wynborough—again!—congratulates the newlyweds and anticipates yet another royal wedding. Stateside sources say Princess Elizabeth may be the next Wyndham bride....

Dear Reader,

Happy New Year to you, and Happy Birthday to us! This year marks the twentieth anniversary of Silhouette Books, and Silhouette Romance is where it all began. Ever since May 1980, Silhouette Romance—and Silhouette Books—has published the best in contemporary category romance fiction, written by the genre's finest authors. And the year's stellar lineups across all Silhouette series continue that tradition.

In Romance this month, bestselling author Stella Bagwell delivers an emotional VIRGIN BRIDES story in which childhood nemeses strike *The Bridal Bargain*. ROYALLY WED, Silhouette's exciting cross-line series, arrives with *The Princess's White Knight* by popular author Carla Cassidy. A rebellious princess, her bodyguard, a marriage of convenience—need I say more? Next month, check out Silhouette Desire's Anne Marie Winston's *The Pregnant Princess* to follow the continuing adventures of the Wyndham family.

Plain Jane Marries the Boss in Elizabeth Harbison's enchanting CINDERELLA BRIDES title. In Donna Clayton's *Adopted Dad*, a first-time father experiences the healing power of love. A small-town beautician becomes *Engaged to the Doctor* to protect her little girl in Robin Nicholas's latest charmer. And *Husband Wanted—Fast!* is a pregnant woman's need in Rebecca Daniels's sparkling Romance.

In coming months, look for special titles by longtime favorites Diana Palmer, Joan Hohl, Kasey Michaels, Dixie Browning, Phyllis Halldorson and Tracy Sinclair, as well as many newer, but just as loved authors. It's an exciting year for Silhouette Books, and we invite you to join the celebration!

Happy reading!

Mary-Theresa Hussey

Mary-Theresa Hussey
Senior Editor

Please address questions and book requests to:
Silhouette Reader Service
U.S.: 3010 Walden Ave., P.O. Box 1325, Buffalo, NY 14269
Canadian: P.O. Box 609, Fort Erie, Ont. L2A 5X3

THE PRINCESS'S WHITE KNIGHT

Carla Cassidy

Silhouette
ROMANCE™
Published by Silhouette Books
America's Publisher of Contemporary Romance

Special thanks and acknowledgment are given to
Carla Cassidy for her contribution to the
Royally Wed series.

To Donna Julian
who yells at me when I don't have dedications.

 SILHOUETTE BOOKS

ISBN 0-373-19415-3

THE PRINCESS'S WHITE KNIGHT

Copyright © 1999 by Harlequin Books S.A.

Visit us at www.romance.net

Printed in U.S.A.

Books by Carla Cassidy

CARLA CASSIDY

is an award-winning author who has written over thirty-five books for Silhouette. In 1995 she won Best Silhouette Romance from *Romantic Times Magazine* for *Anything for Danny*. In 1998, she also won a Career Achievement Award for Best Innovative Series from *Romantic Times Magazine*.

Carla believes the only thing better than curling up with a good book to read is sitting down at the computer with a good story to write. She's looking forward to writing many more books and bringing hours of pleasure to readers.

THE WYNDHAMS

Prince Phillip Wyndham (King of Wynborough)
m.
Gabriella Clark (Queen of Wynborough)

James (presumed dead)	Alexandra m. Mitch Colton	Elizabeth	Katherine m. Trey Sutherland	SERENA m. GABRIEL MORGAN
MAN... MERCENARY... MONARCH	A ROYAL BABY ON THE WAY	THE PREGNANT PRINCESS	UNDERCOVER PRINCESS	THE PRINCESS'S WHITE KNIGHT
Special Edition #1303 on sale February 2000	Special Edition #1281 on sale October 1999	Desire #1268 on sale January 2000	Intimate Moments #968 on sale November 1999	Silhouette Romance #1415 on sale December 1999

Chapter One

He sensed her before he saw her. Her Royal Highness sneaking out of her royal bedroom to get her royal behind in trouble.

Gabriel Morgan frowned as he followed the evocative scent of her perfume down the long hallway that eventually would take him to the living room and the front door of the luxurious vacation home.

The hallway was dark, the house quiet as the rest of the household servants slept. Gabriel heard a thud, then a muffled groan as Princess Serena Wyndham apparently misjudged the length of the hallway and walked into a wall.

Gabriel made no such mistake. He moved with the stealth of a wild animal pursuing prey. Only in this case, his prey was one hundred and ten pounds of utter trouble.

This wasn't the first time she'd attempted to escape the confines of the Aspen family vacation home alone, without her bodyguard. In the months they had been here, Princess Serena had tried to sneak out countless times, and thankfully each time Gabriel had caught her.

He moved into the living room, where the Aspen moon sent bright shafts of ghostly light through the floor-to-ceiling windows. The illumination provided him an easy view of the young woman who crept across the floor toward the front door.

She held a pair of ski boots in hand and she moved slowly, with exaggerated motions in an attempt to make absolutely no noise.

Gabriel waited until she reached up to turn the deadbolt lock. "Going somewhere?" He hit the lights, flooding the room with brilliance.

She squealed and jumped in surprise. Whirling around to face him, she drew a deep breath and Gabriel waited for a display of her royal temper.

"Must you always creep up on me?" Her eyes sparked with obvious ire, the emerald coat she wore a perfect match for their shimmering hue. "Why aren't you in bed?" she demanded. "Don't you ever sleep?"

"Not when you don't," he replied.

She pulled off the ski jacket hood, releasing a spill of red hair, then frowned in irritation. "I was going to step outside for a little breath of fresh air."

"Okay," he agreed. "Just let me get my coat and I'll go with you."

"If I wanted you to go with me, I'd have issued a formal invitation." She dropped the boots to the floor with a thud. She unzipped the ski jacket and shrugged it off, exposing a petite, but shapely body clad in a pair of designer jeans and a bulky beige sweater.

"It's my job to go with you," Gabe said, studiously ignoring how rich and thick her red hair looked against the paleness of the sweater.

"You take your job far too seriously," she exclaimed. She walked over to the sofa and sank down. "I'm going stir-crazy here. It's not fair that my sisters are all off on adventures while I'm stuck here like a baby."

Gabe said nothing, although nobody looked less like a baby than Serena. At twenty-one years old, she might be the youngest of the royal family, but she was definitely all woman.

"Serena, you know your sisters aren't off on lighthearted jaunts. They're seeking clues to your brother's whereabouts."

For a moment Serena seemed to forget her irritation. She leaned toward him, her features soft and wistful. "Oh, Gabe, do you really think it's possible James is still alive after all these years?"

"I don't know. I hope so," he replied.

Prince James Wyndham, the first and only son of Phillip Wyndham, King of Wynborough, had been kidnapped from the town of Aspen twenty-nine years before. Just recently, evidence that he might still be alive and living in the United States had surfaced. Serena and her sisters were determined to discover if their brother was alive and well.

"It would be so wonderful if we could find James

before the celebration of the anniversary of father's coronation.'' Serena sighed, her features softened with longing. ''He'd be thirty years old by now. A big brother.''

Gabe shifted uncomfortably from one foot to the other, unaccustomed to seeing Serena look so subdued and vulnerable. When she looked like this, it made a man want to wrap his arms around her, hold her close and never let her go.

The softness fell away and she glared at Gabe. ''And hopefully he won't be as bossy and overly protective with me as you are.''

Gabe relaxed, much more comfortable and familiar with her irritability where he was concerned. ''Your father expects me to be bossy and overly protective.''

''I don't see why you didn't go with Alexandra and Elizabeth to Arizona, or with Katherine to New Mexico.''

''Both Alexandra and Katherine now have husbands to watch over them, and Elizabeth can take care of herself,'' Gabe replied.

''So can I!'' Serena returned.

Gabe didn't reply. He didn't dare tell her the truth, that of the four princesses, Gabe knew that Serena was the one most likely to find trouble.

Impetuous and willful to a fault, Serena far too often followed her heart and sense of adventure rather than her head and sense of duty.

When the other three sisters had taken off to follow leads about Prince James, Gabe had elected to stick with Serena, knowing that was what King Phillip would want, and Queen Gabriella as well.

Of the four girls, Serena was the one who had inherited not only her mother's red hair and green eyes, but Gabe suspected Serena got her adventurous soul from her beautiful mother as well.

"Do you still want to get some fresh air?" Gabe asked. "I'll take a walk with you if that's what you want."

"Just the kind of thing I dream about...a moonlight walk in the snow with my bodyguard," Serena replied dryly. She covered a yawn with the back of her hand. "I think I'll just go ahead and go to bed." She stood, grabbed her boots and coat and started toward Gabe at the threshold of the hallway.

Instantly he was once again aware of her perfume, a spicy fragrance both arresting and distinct. She stepped so close to him, he could see the tiny flecks of gold that mingled with the green of her eyes. He could feel her body heat, radiating outward to encompass him.

She smiled, a teasing smile that caused a dimple to dance on the left side of her full mouth. "Want to come and tuck me in?" she asked, her voice low and husky.

Although his impulse was to take a step backward, gain distance between her body and his, through sheer willpower alone he remained unmoving, his expression impassive. "Good night, Princess."

For a brief moment, her eyes held the same soft wistfulness they'd had before, then she whirled away from him and down the hallway toward her room.

She paused at her door and turned back to him. "Oh, I forgot to tell you. I've got an interview scheduled at nine tomorrow at a radio station in town. Just another boring publicity engagement." Without waiting for his reply, she went into her room and closed the door.

Gabe narrowed his eyes thoughtfully. Something was up. She'd made her announcement with a studied nonchalance, but he sensed the fidgety energy radiating from her. Besides, all interview requests filtered through him so he could check out the security situation. Laura Bishop, the social secretary for the princesses, would never set up an interview without letting him know about it in advance.

Instead of going back to his room, Gabe stretched out on the sofa where he would be alerted if Serena attempted another escape.

Yes, something was amiss and he had a feeling he'd better be on his toes in the morning. He had a feeling his princess intended to fly the coop, and he had every intention of being by her side.

Serena sank into the airplane seat with a sigh of intense satisfaction. She'd done it. She'd fooled him and very soon she would be on her way to Las Vegas alone, without her handsome, sober bodyguard anywhere in sight.

It had been surprisingly easy. While Gabe had parked the car, Serena had gone into the front of the radio station and out the back door where a cab had been waiting.

Her self-congratulatory smile faded as she thought of Gabriel Morgan.

While she'd been with her sisters, she hadn't paid much attention to their keeper. It had only been since her sisters had left and she and Gabe had been alone in the Aspen vacation home that she'd begun to entertain disturbing thoughts about him.

Lately her thoughts toward Gabe were more than disturbing. During the days, she found herself studying him, wondering about him. And during the nights, she had been having dreams about him, fantasizing an intense, passionate relationship with him.

It wouldn't be so bad if she thought he reciprocated her feelings in any way, but she knew he didn't. He acted as if she were nothing more than a spoiled brat, an immature little girl who needed his presence to stay safe.

She definitely needed to get some distance from him. She needed to get some perspective. Of course she fantasized about him. Other than her father, he was the only male in her life.

A smile once again curved her lips and she slapped on a pair of sunglasses and leaned her head back against the seat.

Las Vegas. It was the perfect place to enjoy some freedom, and in the process she could chase down a lead about James…a lead that had been languishing while she fulfilled her obligations of publicizing the approaching anniversary of her father's coronation.

She eyed the empty seat next to her. Perhaps a handsome young stranger would sit beside her and they would spend the flight time indulging in playful flirting.

Or maybe she'd meet somebody wonderful in Las Vegas. He'd be tall and handsome and he'd fall in love with her not because she was Princess Serena, but just plain Serena, the princess of his heart. She closed her eyes and shivered with excitement.

Surely a couple of days in Las Vegas would put her crazy feelings for Gabe into perspective. And maybe…just maybe…she'd fall desperately, helplessly in love with a man who could fulfill all the romantic fantasies that ached in her heart.

"Going somewhere?"

The deep, familiar voice washed over her with a combination of heat and dread. She opened her eyes and met Gabe's dark gaze. He grinned at her expression of utter disbelief.

He stowed a bag in the overhead compartment, then slid into the seat next to her. Instantly she could smell him. He always smelled like Aspen, like clean mountain air with a whispered breeze of pine.

She snatched off her sunglasses and eyed him in disbelief. "How did you find me? What gave it away? Where did I mess up?" She frowned with irritation. "Tell the truth, you had a homing device surgically implanted in me one night while I slept."

One dark eyebrow rose wryly. "A homing device? Surgical implantation? Princess, you've been watching too much television."

Serena's irritation grew by leaps and bounds. "Of

course I've been watching too much television. That's because I have no life. Eventually, I'll be the oldest living virgin in the world because my body-guard won't give me a moment of privacy.''

She flushed hotly, mortified by the impetuous gallop of her tongue. ''Just…just don't talk to me. Pretend you don't know me at least for the duration of this flight.'' She grabbed a magazine from her over-size purse and flipped it open on her lap, embarrassed and determined to ignore him for as long as possible.

''As you like it, Princess,'' he murmured, then leaned his head back and closed his eyes.

He'd even brought a suitcase, Serena thought as she stared down at the magazine in her lap. He'd known she was catching a flight and had been completely prepared. The man was positively amazing.

She cast him a surreptitious glance. As always, he was the epitome of a well-groomed male. He wore a navy suit with her family crest embroidered on the breast of the jacket. His dark hair was neat, his jaw without a shadow of an errant whisker. With his eyes closed, she had full view of his sinfully long lashes.

Serena's sister, Elizabeth, had once declared that Gabe had bedroom eyes, the kind that made women think of breathless kisses and tangled sheets and heated caresses.

Bedroom eyes and a cold, unemotional heart. Heaven help the woman who falls in love with Gabriel Morgan, Serena thought. She gazed once again at her magazine, more determined than ever to ignore the handsome man beside her.

She'd been so certain she'd done it this time, successfully made her escape from him. How had he known? How had he managed not only to catch this flight, but also to be prepared enough to have a bag packed?

She had to know where she'd made her mistake...had to know so the next time she wouldn't repeat it. "You have to tell me how you knew I was going to try to sneak away," she finally said.

She stared at him, waiting for an answer. He didn't move, didn't twitch an eyelid. She sighed impatiently. "It's only fair that you tell me."

He opened his eyes and gazed at her blankly. "Excuse me, ma'am, are you talking to me?"

Serena grimaced, remembering the last thing she'd said to him was for him to pretend he didn't know her for the duration of the flight. The man was utterly maddening. "Gabriel, please. Just tell me how you knew."

He smiled, a smug, slightly superior smile that made Serena want to scream. "There were a dozen clues that let me know you had something planned. Clue number one..." He shifted in his chair and held up a finger. His leg pressed warmly against hers. "You never set up your own interviews. Laura does that for you.

"Clue number two..." A second finger joined the first. "All morning you vibrated with energy. Every gesture, every movement signaled something was going to happen."

He lowered his hand to his knee. "A word of advice, Princess. While in Las Vegas, you'd do well to stay away from the poker tables. You don't exactly possess a poker face." He grinned. "And you don't bluff well at all."

"But how did you know about the flight? About Las Vegas?" she asked, trying to stay focused on the conversation and not on his overwhelming nearness.

He shrugged. "I called Laura first thing this morning. She told me she'd booked tickets on this flight. Of course, she'd booked two because she didn't know you intended to ditch me and come alone."

Serena nodded thoughtfully. She should have known better than to make all her arrangements through Laura, but old habits died hard and it never crossed her mind to make the travel arrangements herself. Next time she'd know better.

"Now, can I ask you a question?" he inquired.

"What?"

"Why Las Vegas? You could have gone anywhere in the country or joined one of your sisters."

Serena frowned. "Remember when Katherine called me and told me about a woman named Betty Jo Parker?" Katherine was one of Serena's older sisters, who had recently married Trey Sutherland, a wealthy CEO in New Mexico.

Gabe frowned. "Vaguely. Doesn't she have something to do with Bill Lewis?" he asked.

Serena nodded. She knew Gabe hadn't followed too closely the sisters' progress in the search for their brother. "Yes, but we don't know what. All we know is that we think Bill Lewis might really be James, and that a woman named Betty Jo Parker tried to reach him at Trey's from a Las Vegas phone number."

"So, you decided to go to Las Vegas and see if you can find this Betty Jo Parker."

"Exactly," she replied. "And hopefully Betty Jo can tell us where Bill is, and hopefully Bill is really James."

"There's a lot of hopefullys in there. You aren't a private investigator, you're a princess," he reminded her gruffly.

"I don't see why I can't be a little of both," she returned. "I've spent the last several months doing every radio and talk show in and around the Aspen area. I have more than done my publicity duty. Now I want to take an active part in the search for my brother."

"Won't your parents wonder what's up when none of you are doing any publicity?" Gabe asked. "That is the reason you gave them for the four of you coming to the States."

Serena waved her hands dismissively. "I've already told Laura to set up some interviews for me in and around the Las Vegas area. I also told her to tell Mother and Father that I'd saturated the Aspen market and thought Las Vegas might be fun."

Gabe grunted and closed his eyes once again. Serena gazed at him for a long moment. Drat, but the man was handsome as the devil.

She wished her father had assigned her a bodyguard who was old, far too old to evoke the kind of fantasies Serena found herself constantly entertaining about Gabe.

She wished her father had hired somebody who didn't have intriguing, haunting secrets in his dark eyes, a man who didn't have shoulders quite so broad, a man who didn't make her knees grow weak with strange emotions that both frightened and disturbed her.

She settled back in her seat and closed her eyes. What she'd told him about wanting to chase down the lead concerning Betty Jo Parker had been true.

However, Las Vegas held an additional draw. Las Vegas...the city of bright lights, fast money and hundreds of wedding chapels.

Wedding chapels. She'd heard that in Las Vegas they came in all shapes and sizes and no blood test or waiting period was required for marriage.

Every year thousands of couples gazed into each other's eyes, spoke their marriage vows and began their lives together as man and wife.

Maybe while she was hunting for the elusive Betty Jo Parker, she would meet a handsome stranger, and in the instant of their eyes meeting, she'd know he was the one for her. Maybe when she finally left Las Vegas, she would no longer be a lonely princess, but rather somebody's cherished wife.

She opened one eye and cast a sideways glance at Gabe. Of course, it would be impossible to indulge in a whirlwind romance, to lose herself in breathtaking spontaneous passion with him as a sidekick.

As the plane engines whined alive, Serena felt a thrum of excitement build inside her. Las Vegas was a big little city. Surely it was big enough for her to lose one handsome, irritating, overzealous body-guard.

Chapter Two

Las Vegas. Energy surged through Gabe as he stood two steps behind Serena on the automated walkway in the Las Vegas airport.

He had a feeling his time of guarding Serena in Aspen would seem like a vacation compared to this. People clogged the walkways...businessmen, vacationers, honeymoon couples...so many people. Late December was the height of the city's tourist season, and it showed.

Although most of the time his biggest challenge was to guard Serena from herself and her crazy impulses, Gabe never lost sight of the fact that she was a princess and, therefore, a potential target. The Wyndhams were already painfully aware of that reality.

Kidnapping a princess would probably yield a criminal a sizable fortune; holding her hostage for partisan gain would be equally appealing to many political zealots.

And Las Vegas was a hotbed of all kinds of humanity in all sizes and shapes. He patted his gun, nestled in its shoulder holster beneath his jacket. The feel of the weapon assured him, although since being in charge of Serena's safety, he'd never had to remove it from its holster.

He hoped they wouldn't be here long. Serena was determined to find Betty Jo Parker, and Gabe would do everything he could to help her in the effort. Within a day or two he wanted to get Serena back to either the family vacation home in Aspen, or back to her parents in Wynborough.

As a former cop, he'd once prided himself on his investigative skills. But that had been almost four years ago…before a bank robbery gone awry had scarred forever the heart of the man he might have been.

He shook his head to dislodge thoughts of the past and instead focused on the woman in front of him, and the surrounding people. He couldn't help but notice the admiring glances Serena received from the males who passed her.

And why wouldn't she draw admiring, even lustful, glances? The green suit she wore was a perfect foil for her flaming hair. The short skirt displayed a sinful length of sexy legs and hugged her slender, but shapely hips. The bolero-type jacket emphasized her tiny waist and the swell of her breasts.

Gabe frowned. His job would be a hell of a lot easier if Serena would wear plastic garbage bags from head to toe, hiding the curves that seemed to beg attention. Unfortunately, Serena had an unerring fashion sense and knew exactly what styles emphasized her attributes.

A car awaited them outside the airport. Gabe slid into the front seat with the driver while Serena was alone in the luxurious rear interior. "Lucky Diamond Hotel," Gabe told the driver, knowing that was where Laura had made the reservations for their indefinite stay in Las Vegas.

The hotel was one of the new ones on the strip, a monolith of glass and steel that towered against the desert sky. It took only minutes for Serena and Gabe to be whisked by a courteous hotel employee to one of the lavish penthouse suites.

Gabe took the smaller of the two bedrooms, although he knew his nights would be spent on the sofa near the front door where he could hear if his charge attempted to sneak away.

The center room was elegant with plush rose carpeting, expensive furniture and a fully stocked wet bar in one corner. An extravagant bouquet of flowers sat on the marble coffee table, alongside a fruit basket that could feed a small village. Both compliments of the hotel.

Gabe stored his clothes in the closet in the bedroom, then went back into the living room, awaiting Serena's next move.

He walked over to the wet bar and eyed a bottle of scotch, waiting to hear the siren call he'd once not been able to ignore. Nothing. No evocative whispered promise of oblivion, no sweet song offering the numbness from pain.

He fixed himself a soft drink, satisfied that his destructive tendencies were truly behind him. Somehow in the past three years, he'd managed to regain some enjoyment in life and his self-respect.

And much of his recovery was due to Serena's father, King Phillip. Gabe owed his life, his sanity and his renewed feeling of worthiness to the king, and in return, he had pledged his honor and his commitment to that same man. And that was why Gabe took his job guarding King Phillip's youngest daughter most seriously.

"Isn't it magnificent?"

Gabe turned away from the bar to see Serena standing at the floor-to-ceiling window that gave a stunning view of sin city and the surrounding desert.

"There's no place like it on this earth," he replied.

She turned and looked at him, curiosity evident in her gaze. "Have you been here before?"

He nodded, remembering a honeymoon suite, a young woman with laughing brown eyes, and a night of promised love forever. Only in their case, forever had lasted less than six months. "Once," he finally answered. "A very long time ago."

She stared at him for another long moment, as if wanting to pursue the topic further. He wasn't sure if it was his forbidding expression or the edge that had been in his voice that changed her mind.

"I'm starving," she said and looked at her watch.

"You want me to call up room service?" he asked.

She eyed him as if he'd lost his mind. "Do you really think I'm going to spend my time in Las Vegas cooped up in this room?"

"One could only hope," he replied dryly.

"Where's your sense of adventure?" she asked, her eyes sparkling with excitement. She turned back to peer out the window, her body appearing to vibrate with the restless energy he'd come to dread. "Oh, this is going to be such fun," she exclaimed.

"Yeah, fun," Gabe echoed with sardonic amusement.

She whirled away from the window and to the front door of the room. "You know, you're welcome to stay right here and catch a nap or grab some room service. I'm sure I'll be just fine on my own."

"Fat chance," Gabe exclaimed, and followed her out the door.

He wasn't surprised when she found one of the biggest buffets in the world at Circus Circus. As she went through the food line, he walked just behind her, watching in indulgent amusement as she piled food high and heavy on her plate.

From the first moment he'd been assigned as a bodyguard and had watched Serena eat, it had amazed him how a woman so petite could eat like a burly ranch hand. Unlike so many women, Serena seemed not to have to watch her weight. He had a feeling she probably burned excess calories in thinking of ways to aggravate him.

By the time Serena left the buffet line, she had

two full plates of food and hadn't yet hit the desserts. Gabe carried his plate and followed her to a couple of empty tables. As she slid into a chair at one of them, he started to sit down at the table next to hers.

"You might as well join me," she said, and motioned him over with a wave of her hand. He changed directions and settled in the chair directly across from her.

For a few minutes they ate in silence. Gabe watched the crowd around them, trying not to focus on Serena. But his gaze was drawn again and again to her.

She was the most sensual eater he'd ever seen. She took obvious pleasure in each morsel, not hesitating to lick her fingers or run her tongue across her bottom lip to capture an errant crumb.

She'd surprised him when she'd spoken of being afraid she'd become the oldest living virgin in Wynborough. He'd suspected she was a virgin due more to circumstance than any commitment on her part to save herself for marriage.

In the two years Gabe had worked for King Phillip, other than the official dates arranged by the palace, Serena didn't appear to have any special suitor.

Gabe envied the man who would be her first lover. He had a feeling Serena would approach lovemaking as she did everything else in her life...with lustful enthusiasm.

"Hmmm, now all I need to top this off is a piece of that sinful chocolate cake," she said as she wiped her mouth with a napkin.

"I'll get it for you, Princess." Gabe jumped up, suddenly feeling the need to distance himself, not so much from her, but rather his own crazy thoughts where she was concerned.

The last thing he needed to do was to entertain fantasies of himself as her first lover. Harboring any such thoughts made him feel disloyal to King Phillip.

Besides the fact that she was his princess and he was her humble protector, there was also the fact that he'd sworn to himself long ago that no woman would ever again possess any piece of his heart.

He grabbed a slice of the requested chocolate cake and carried it back to the table, the short walk and stern self-admonishment working to put him back in a proper mindset.

"Here you are, Princess," he said as he placed the cake before her.

He sat back down and nodded to the waiter who appeared as if by magic at their table to refill their coffee cups. As Serena polished off the cake, he kept his focus studiously away from her and on the people coming and going at the tables nearby.

She had just finished her cake when an elderly woman who'd been sitting at the table next to them leaned over and touched Serena's shoulder. From caution borne of bitter experience, Gabe's hand automatically went beneath his jacket to his gun.

"I couldn't help but overhear the two of you while I was eating," the older woman said. She smiled, a sweet gesture that wreathed her face with wrinkles. "My William, God rest his soul, used to call me Princess."

Gabe relaxed, sensing no danger. The woman turned to Gabe, her smile deepening. "It's so nice to hear a young man talking so sweetly to his lady. It's obvious the two of you are very much in love."

"Oh, but I'm not—" Gabe grunted as Serena's foot connected solidly with his shin beneath the table.

Serena smiled and grabbed Gabe's hand. Her dimple flashed at the corner of her mouth with her impish smile. "He loves me madly and passionately, just as I love him."

Her thumb caressed the back of his hand, shooting rivulets of warmth up his arm. She leaned closer to the older woman. "He not only calls me Princess, he treats me like one. Don't you, darling?" Her eyes glittered with mischief.

"Oh, that's wonderful." The old woman clapped her hands together in delight. "I hope the two of you have many happy years together, just like my William and I did."

"Trust me, I don't intend to let him go for a very long time," Serena replied and she raised Gabe's hand to her lips. She pressed her mouth against the back of his hand in a sensual kiss. Her gaze never left his, as if she wanted to see what response her kiss would bring.

The rivulets of warmth that had been racing through him ignited into flames. The heat her kiss had evoked was bewitching…addictive.

With a happy nod to them both, the old woman

murmured goodbye, then rose and walked away. The minute her back was turned, Gabe snatched his hand from Serena's, irritated with her for her teasing, and irritated with himself for his response. She laughed, as if aware that he'd not been unaffected by her touch.

"How do you plan on finding this Betty Jo Parker?" he asked, wanting to remind her of the reason she was here and get his own mind away from her kiss.

"I've got her phone number and an address back at the room. But I don't intend to do anything about that today. I'll start the search first thing in the morning." She smiled with excitement. "Today I just want to wallow in the experience of Las Vegas." She pushed away from the table and stood. "And the first thing I need to do is walk off this incredible meal."

Gabe followed her out of the restaurant, trying desperately not to notice the sway of her hips, trying desperately to forget the sweet warmth of her lips against his skin.

She was a tease, a young woman experiencing her first flush of sexual awareness. At twenty-one years old, Serena appeared to be researching the power of her female wiles...and they were powerful.

He frowned with irritation. His biggest problem at the moment was in protecting Serena from herself and her adventurous soul. He hoped that it never came to a situation where he had to protect her from himself.

* * *

She'd irritated him. As Serena left Circus Circus and walked out into the warm desert air, she was aware of Gabe following close behind her, his dark eyebrows pulled together in a scowl. Like an angry pit bull, he looked as if he might take a bite out of anyone who approached too near.

She knew she'd irritated him with her teasing game with the old woman. But it was his own fault. She'd asked him again and again not to call her Princess, but rather to use her name, Serena. But Gabe continued to be proper. A proper, uptight, stick-in-the-mud.

All she wanted was to experience life, not as a princess, but as a normal, healthy twenty-one year old. A normal, healthy twenty-one year old who had spent most of her life desperately lonely.

She halted and waited for him to catch up with her. "I'm sorry if I embarrassed you before," she said.

He eyed her in surprise. "No problem," he replied, but her apology did nothing to remove his frown.

"Is it possible you could lose the scowl?" she asked. "You know, could you maybe look pleased to be here?"

"It'd be a stretch," he returned. "I'm not exactly pleased to be here."

"Why not?" she asked incredulously. "I'd think you'd appreciate the break from the boredom of being cooped up in the house in Aspen."

His dark gaze played over her face. "I'm not particularly happy to be here because I don't trust you at all.''

She worked for an expression of surprise, but it was simply out of her reach. She stopped walking and turned to face him. She knew exactly why he didn't trust her and he had every reason not to. "Okay...what if I agree to be good for today, if I promise no attempt to get away from you...would that earn a smile?"

To her delight, the corners of his lips turned up ever so slightly and the darkness of his eyes lightened a bit. "It would have to be a cross-your-heart, hope-to-die kind of promise before I'd really believe it.''

She made an imaginary cross over her heart. "Cross my heart and hope to die, I won't try to get away from you for the remainder of the day. I promise, and I never, ever break my promises. Now, will you lose the pit bull expression?"

"Pit bull?" A burst of laughter escaped him. "Is that what I look like to you?"

The sound of his deep, melodic laughter filled her with warmth.

When he scowled, he was still handsome, but when he laughed, he was absolutely devastating. He made her want to melt against him, curl up in his arms and feel that rumble of laughter vibrate inside his chest.

She felt an unaccustomed blush warm her cheeks. Her thoughts irritated her. Somehow she had to stop her crazy musings about Gabe. He was her bodyguard, and to her dismay, he'd never given her any sign that he wanted to be anything more to her.

"Okay, so it's settled," she said briskly. "For the rest of the day you won't glower and glare at people and you'll pretend you enjoy being here."

"I'll do the best I can, Princess," he replied, amused indulgence lighting his eyes.

"And don't call me Princess," she exclaimed. She took a step closer to him, wondering if it was the desert warmth she felt or his body heat radiating out to encompass her.

She reached out a hand and placed it on his arm. "Gabe, please. I've asked you a dozen times in the past, but it's really important to me that I be as inconspicuous as possible. I don't want people to know who I am. I just want to be a regular person. For the duration of our stay in Las Vegas, I don't want to be Princess Serena. I just want to be Serena."

"I'll do the best I can," he agreed, any smile gone from him. She felt the tension in his arm and dropped her hand. She knew he didn't like to be touched. Any simple touch from her always made his eyes darken and his muscles bunch as if in protest. And that was exactly why she wanted to get away from him, to find a man who'd long for her touch.

"Good, so it's settled. I'm Serena for as long as we're here." She began walking once again, Gabe at her side. She'd promised him she would be good for today, and she'd told the truth. She wouldn't try to lose him. But at midnight, her promise would expire.

"Oh look, a street musician." She pointed ahead of them, where a man with a guitar was singing and strumming, entertaining the crowd that had gathered around him.

Just what she needed, a diversion from her preoccupation with Gabe. She wiggled her way toward the front of the enthusiastic audience, aware of Gabe trailing in back of her.

She tapped her foot in time to the music and tried to stay focused on the entertainer, but it was difficult to focus on anything but Gabe's body directly behind hers. If she leaned back just a little, she would be nestled intimately against him. She closed her eyes for a moment, weak with temptation.

But she knew what would happen. She'd feel him tense in protest, and he'd quickly step aside, breaking immediately any intimate contact between them.

When the singer ended his song, the crowd began to disperse. Serena had only taken a couple of steps away when a little girl tugged at the bottom of her skirt.

Serena smiled at the child, who looked to be no older than six and had a riotous burst of blond curls all over her head. Serena loved children. She hoped someday to have a dozen of her own.

"Hi, sweetheart," she said to the young girl.

"My mommy says you're a real princess. Can I have your autograph?" she asked. She held out a slip of paper and a pen.

At that moment, the child's mother approached,

an expression of awe on her face. "We're sorry to bother you," the woman said. "I recognize you from the interview you did in *Today's Woman,* and I told my Samantha that you were a princess and perhaps you'd give her an autograph."

"I'd be honored to," Serena replied, although she was dismayed at being recognized. She took the pen and paper the girl held out and quickly signed her name. "There you are, sweetheart," she said to little Samantha.

"Thank you," Samantha said shyly.

"Samantha is a very pretty name," she said and was rewarded by a smile.

"Someday I want to grow up and be a princess," Samantha said.

As the mother and child moved away, Serena stared after them. She sighed and began to walk once again. "Every little girl wants to grow up to be a princess. I wonder if every princess wants to grow up to be just an ordinary girl?"

"Is that what you wish?" Gabe asked.

"Sometimes," she admitted. "I just wish for a little while I could be an average young woman. I wish I could go out with somebody and not have to worry about if he's with me for political gain, or to please the press. I wish..." She broke off, unwilling to share her innermost dreams with a man who was with her because of duty to her father. "Never mind," she said, and waved her hand to dismiss the entire conversation.

She couldn't tell Gabe that what she most wished for was marriage and babies, a life filled with love and laughter rather than pomp and circumstance. And she definitely couldn't confess that when she indulged in daydreams, they always included him.

"What about you? Don't you ever get tired of having no life other than mine?" she asked him. "I mean, if I want Chinese food, that's what you eat. If I want to see a movie, that's what you see. Everything you do revolves around my choices, my schedule."

"That's my job," he returned easily.

"But that's not a life," she protested.

"My job is my life," he said with more vehemence than her protest required. He smiled, as if in an attempt to lighten his intensity. "When I pledged myself to your father and his reign, I gave up all rights to any personal life."

Serena gazed at him for a long moment, seeking answers in his handsome features. But he gave nothing away. Why would a man with Gabe's looks, his obvious intelligence, pledge himself so completely to another and sacrifice all personal choice and freedom?

She walked into a casino and sat down at one of the dollar slot machines. Gabe sat at the one next to her and twirled his chair around so he could survey anyone who might come too near.

She fed a twenty-dollar bill into the slot and twenty dollar tokens clunked into the bin. She'd never been much of a gambler. What she really wanted to do was sit and get to know a little bit more about Gabe. She actually knew very little about the man who occupied her fantasies, the man whom her father had entrusted with her very life. The right moment to ask personal questions had never presented itself. They were rarely alone and the few times they had been alone, she'd found herself ridiculously shy and tongue-tied by the childish crush she'd entertained. But she was no longer a child and she refused to consider that what she felt for Gabe had anything to do with a simple silly crush.

"What did you do before you came to work for my father?" she asked him. She put a token in the machine and hit the button to spin the reel.

"Nothing that would interest a princess," he replied. His voice held a tiny note of tension that let her know he found her question an intrusion.

That didn't stop her from pursuing the issue. "If you won't tell me, I'll just have to guess." She turned her chair and eyed him boldly. "I think probably you were either a gangster or a hit man."

She was rewarded with his burst of laughter and amusement lighting the darkness of his eyes. "A hit man? You have definitely been watching too much television." His laughter died and shadows once again usurped the momentary glow of his eyes. "I was a police officer before I came to work for your father."

"A police officer?" Somehow it didn't surprise her. She had suspected a background in either law enforcement or the military. Her father wouldn't have hired anyone without some sort of professional training.

She gave up all pretense of playing the machine

and instead focused her full attention on him. "Where? I mean, what city in the States?"

"Kansas City, Missouri," he answered grudgingly, as if somehow he were giving away pieces of himself that could never be retrieved.

"Is that where your family is? In Kansas City?"

"What is this? Twenty questions?" he asked, a touch of irritation back in his voice.

"I just suddenly realized that I don't know anything about you," she replied, refusing to be distracted from what had become a mission. "So, is it?" she pressed.

He sighed in resignation. "I don't have any family. I prefer rock to classical music, steak to seafood and action movies to dramas. There, now you know everything that's worth knowing about me." He looked away from her, once again studying their surroundings.

She frowned at him, instinctively knowing there was much, much more to the man than he offered. There were secrets in his eyes, a profound sadness that sometimes radiated from him.

"What was a police officer from Kansas City, Missouri, doing in Wynborough?" She knew part of the story that had brought Gabe to her father's attention.

King Phillip had been about to make a public speech when Gabe, who had been in the audience, spied a man with a gun. Instantly, Gabe had wrestled the man to the ground and gained possession of the gun, saving the king's life. Soon after, Gabe had been offered the position of head of palace security before being assigned as head of the Royal Wynborough Bodyguards.

"I wasn't a police officer anymore when I came to Wynborough." Again, there was an edge of tension in his voice.

"So, what were you doing in Wynborough?"

He hesitated a moment, then replied, "Vacation. I was on vacation."

"Aren't you ever lonely, Gabe?" she asked softly. Didn't he ever long for somebody to hold, somebody to love?

His gaze swung back to her and he emitted a dry laugh. "Lonely? Since you became my charge, I don't have the time and I'm never alone long enough to get lonely."

Serena turned back to her machine and fed in several more coins one at a time as she mulled over his words. It was true, he was virtually never alone, and yet in many ways he was always alone.

She looked at him once again. "I know you spend all your time with me, but you're still alone. I mean, we're together...but not really." She frowned, aware that she wasn't clearly communicating what she really meant.

Gabe's life was every bit as confined as hers due to their stations, hers as a princess and his as a royal bodyguard. He couldn't date, couldn't just take off on a whim and see a movie or eat out. His every move was dictated by hers, and her every move was usually dictated by her duty.

"Don't you ever wish for somebody to share your

heart? Somebody you could tell your dreams?'' Do you ever think of me? her heart yearned to ask.

"Never," he said succinctly. "Besides—" he offered her a thin smile "—I don't waste time entertaining dreams, and I definitely don't have a heart."

Serena gazed at him for a long moment. She didn't believe him. She didn't know what his past experiences had been, but somewhere along the road of his life, he'd abandoned his dreams and closed off his heart.

But lost dreams could be found, and a closed heart could be reopened. Love could accomplish all those things and more.

She had a feeling that the woman who managed to tap into Gabe's dreams, to step into his heart, would be the luckiest woman alive.

What she didn't know was if she was the woman to accomplish such a task. She didn't know if she should run from him, escape and fly solo to find the love her heart craved. Or should she stay with him, spend time with him, and hope she could be the woman who would reawaken his dreams, his love.

It was a gamble either way. She fed the last of her coins into the slot machine and hit the button to spin the reel. Nothing. She'd never been very lucky at gambling.

Chapter Three

Gabe hadn't lied to her. He'd lost his dreams a long time ago, and he'd locked away his heart at the same time, building barriers around it that would keep it safe and untouched.

He'd first learned to guard his heart while still a boy. As a foster child, he'd learned not to love too much, too deeply, that nothing and nobody could be counted on forever.

He'd allowed the barriers to drop only once, and the result had devastated him. He wouldn't make the same mistake again.

Serena had irritated him with her probing questions. She'd made him think about people, places and times he didn't want to remember.

As he followed her down the sidewalk once again, he reminded himself that she was young, a complete stranger to tragedy, an innocent to the cruel winds of fate.

She was still young enough to believe in the power of love and the concept of soul mates. She had yet to taste the bitter tang of regret, experience the utter emptiness of loss. And he hoped she never would.

Eventually he knew Serena would probably marry a prince. She would set up a household in a castle with all the trappings of her station, and fulfill the duties she was born for.

He frowned, wondering why the thought of Serena happily married rankled him. It was probably because he knew until that happened, he was responsible for her. And being responsible for Serena was a momentous task.

Apparently his terse reply concerning his dreams and his heart had momentarily stifled her curiosity about him. She'd stopped asking questions and instead had grown quiet and introspective.

There were times when he found her endless chattering rather trying, but her silence worried him far more. When Serena grew quiet, it usually meant she was thinking, and rarely did anything good come from that.

She had been right about one thing. The moment he'd become a royal bodyguard, he'd given up all rights to his own life. He no longer made the decisions a normal man made. His decisions were made by Serena, who set the daily schedule and he merely followed.

He'd learned to snooze when she slept, shower while she showered, and constantly be aware of her and her safety. His every move was dictated by hers and for the moment it was a life-style that suited him perfectly. He had little time for thinking of anything other than his duty to King Phillip and how to remain one step ahead of Serena.

"Oh, Gabe, look!" The object of his thoughts grabbed his arm and pointed to a building across the street. The building, a traditional gray stone chapel, was nearly lost between two towering, glittering casinos.

The only concession to the surrounding tourism and capitalism was a bright gold banner that proclaimed the place Ye Olde Wedding Chapel.

"Let's go inside," she said, her features shining with excitement.

Gabe wanted to protest. He didn't want to enter any chapel for any reason. But, of course, it wasn't his place to lodge any complaint. With a long-suffering sigh, he followed her into the front door.

There was nothing traditional about the lobby area. A sign posted the prices of a variety of different kinds of wedding ceremonies. A refrigerated unit against one wall held fresh flower arrangements, the bouquets in a variety of sizes and styles, with different colored ribbons to match each assortment of blooms.

Dozens of wedding photos decorated the wall opposite the floral display, each with a smiling couple and a bald minister with a bulbous nose.

Serena peeked through the window in the door that led to the inner sanctum of the church. She turned back to Gabe, her eyes dazzling bright. "There's a couple in there getting married right now." She grabbed his hand. "Come on, let's go in and watch."

Again, Gabe fought a protest, unsure if he wanted to complain about her plan to watch a wedding or reprove her for holding his hand, the connection both warm and unsettling.

They entered through the door and Serena led him to the back pew, where they eased down, their presence not interrupting the ceremony in progress.

Gabe wanted his hand back, but Serena held tight. The minister was reading a section of the Bible, but Gabe had trouble focusing on the man's words. His head was filled with the scent of Serena, the evocative spicy scent that she always wore.

"They probably met in a nightclub several nights ago," Serena whispered, her gaze not leaving the couple who had begun to exchange their vows. "It was love at first sight, and they've spent every moment together since."

Her hand tightened around Gabe's. "Maybe he's a school principal and she's a teacher, and they have everything in common and this is the beginning of a wonderful life for them, a life filled with love and happiness."

"He's probably a hardware salesman from Toledo and she's a waitress. Their marriage will probably last no longer than six months before they both realize this wedding was a big mistake," Gabe said. "These quickie weddings almost never last." He stifled a yelp as Serena pinched him.

"You stop it right now, Gabriel Morgan," she hissed beneath her breath. She glared at him, her eyes green crystals of ice. "Don't you dare say another word to ruin my fantasy." She looked back at the "happy" couple and her features softened. "Look at them," she said. "He loves her desperately, hopelessly, as she loves him."

Gabe followed her gaze, grudgingly admitting the two people did appear to be in love. As the groom placed a ring on his intended's finger, Gabe remembered doing the same in a distant past.

LeAnn hadn't worn white. She'd worn a vivid pink suit, refusing to be confined by tradition. They'd married right here in Vegas, the culmination of an eight-week whirlwind romance. They'd had six months together as man and wife before fate had intervened.

Funny, the intense pain that thoughts of LeAnn had always brought with them was finally gone. He closed his eyes and tried to conjure a picture of her in his mind.

Instead of LeAnn's blond hair, his mind filled with the vision of a cascade of fiery red curls, green eyes, sparking with fire and passion, and inviting lips, parted as if waiting for his kiss.

Serena.

Damn. He snapped his eyes open and extricated his hand from hers. At that moment the minister pronounced the couple man and wife and the newlyweds shared a kiss.

Gabe looked at Serena, surprised to find her eyes filled with tears. She caught his gaze and emitted an embarrassed little laugh. "I know…it's crazy," she said as she swiped her tears with her fingers. "I don't even know them, but I'm so happy for them."

Oddly, her tears moved him. He pulled a clean handkerchief from his pocket and handed it to her. Serena rarely wept, and it touched him that she could so easily cry tears of joy for strangers. "Don't be embarrassed," he replied. "Lots of people cry at weddings."

"Let's get out of here," she said.

They snuck out of the chapel just ahead of the newly wedded couple and for the next couple of hours wandered the strip, sightseeing with the rest of the tourists. Serena was quiet, her thoughts obviously far away from the glittering casinos with their dazzling designs.

Gabe was grateful when she spied a casino offering a prime rib special, and decided to get a bite to eat.

"You aren't really such a cynic about love, are you?" she asked when they were seated at a secluded table in the dimly lit dining area.

He shrugged, finding it difficult to look at her. The glow of the candle in the center of the table stroked her like a lover, pulling soft color into her cheeks and accentuating the brilliant green of her eyes. "I'm not necessarily a cynic about love, but I do doubt the longevity of quickie Las Vegas marriages."

"But why? Love doesn't know where or in what kind of ceremony you get married."

He smiled. "True, but if I was to make an educated guess, I'd surmise that most of the Las Vegas weddings take place due to lust, rather than love.''

"I'd settle for a little lust in my life at this point," she said and gave him a sly glance as if to gauge his reaction.

He knew she expected a stern admonishment. He didn't give it to her. "Trust me, Princess, lust is vastly overrated.''

She eyed him curiously. "You sound like you're no stranger to lust." She leaned forward, so close the warmth of her breath stirred past the candle flame and caressed his face. "Tell me who you lusted for...what kind of woman she was.''

Gabe wanted to change the subject, felt the suffocating crush of ancient regrets pressing hard against his chest. He wished there was some way to divert her from the question, but she had the look of a determined hound dog with the scent of prey in her nose and he knew nothing would satisfy her except answers.

He leaned back in his chair and eyed her with studied indulgence. "She was a gorgeous blonde with big blue eyes and a laugh that made me feel all warm inside.''

Serena nodded, as if to encourage him to confide further in her. "And did you love her desperately?''

"Madly, passionately," he said, trying not to notice how utterly appealing Serena looked. There was a wistful softness in her eyes, a slight tremble to her lips. And in that moment, Gabe wanted her as he'd never wanted a woman before.

"What happened?" she asked.

He shrugged. "Her parents moved away and she had to go with them. She was only in third grade. I was in fourth."

He watched in satisfaction as the soft wistfulness in her eyes died, replaced by exasperation.

"You're making fun of me," she said. She leaned back in her chair and ran her hands over the napkin in her lap. The tremble of her lips was more pronounced, only this time in hurt.

Instantly Gabe wanted to lean across the table, stroke her arm or touch her face and say he was sorry. But the waiter arrived with their food, and the moment was lost.

Just as well, he thought, as they began to eat their meal in silence. He was beginning to realize that there was no way he could touch Serena and not feel desire. Somehow, she'd begun to crawl under his skin.

Tomorrow they would seek out Betty Jo Parker, then Gabe would escort Princess Serena back to her parents in Wynborough. And once in Wynborough, Gabe would ask for a transfer of duty. In time, he would forget the crazy, inappropriate desire that one certain red-haired minx had managed to stir.

When Serena awoke the next morning, the desert sun had already crept halfway up the sky. "Rats," she muttered as she grabbed the alarm clock on the nightstand. "Double rats," she exclaimed as she saw it was nearly ten o'clock.

Minutes later, she stood beneath a hot shower, cursing the good night's sleep she'd gained. After dinner, she and Gabe had attended one of the Las Vegas shows, a glittering extravaganza that had been both beautiful and entertaining.

However, she'd had found it difficult to stay focused on the merriment on stage. Gabe's presence in the seat next to hers was distracting. He was easily the most handsome man at the show, and she couldn't help but notice the admiring gazes he drew from other women.

She remained aloof throughout the show, still smarting from the way he'd teased her about lust and love. When they returned to their hotel, she'd gone directly to her bedroom with every intention of sneaking out after midnight and experiencing life far away from his domineering, overly protective manner. Unfortunately, her body had betrayed her and almost immediately she'd fallen asleep.

She finished her shower, dressed and blow-dried her hair, then left her room and went into the main area of the suite.

Gabe was there at the table, sipping a cup of coffee and reading the morning newspaper. As she came into the room, he stood and reached for his jacket, which hung on the back of his chair.

"Relax," she said and waved him back down. "I'm not going anywhere or doing anything until I have a cup of coffee."

"There are sweet rolls and muffins there, too," he said, and pointed to the room service cart, then returned his focus to the paper.

Serena poured herself a cup of coffee and grabbed

a huge cinnamon roll, then sat at the table in the chair opposite Gabe.

As she ate her roll, she studied Gabe's features, trying to figure out what it was about the man that so attracted her to him. Granted, he was handsome, with his dark brown hair and chiseled features. But she'd attended royal functions with other handsome men dancing attendance on her. She'd dated princes and dukes, viscounts and barons. For the most part they'd been handsome men with impeccable manners who had bored her to tears.

No, it wasn't just Gabe's looks that drew her to him. It was an aura of suppressed danger that radiated from him, a proficiency in dealing with any and all situations that might arise. More than this, it was the streak of humor he infrequently exhibited, the spark of emotion that sometimes lit his features, and those haunting dark shadows that at times eclipsed the light in his eyes.

He raised an eyebrow at her. "I would think a princess would know that it's rude to stare."

An embarrassed blush warmed her cheeks, but she didn't avert her gaze from him. "And I would think a bodyguard would know that it's rude to remind a princess of her shortcomings."

"Touché," he said, the corner of his mouth curling up in a smile of amusement. He got up to pour himself a fresh cup of coffee. When he turned back to face her, she noticed the top two buttons of his shirt were unfastened, allowing curly dark chest hairs to escape over the top of the crisp cotton confines.

Her mind filled with a vision of her hands dancing in that hair, reveling in the coarse tendrils curling around her fingers, tickling her nose as she pressed her lips against the center of his chest.

"So, what are your plans for the day?" he asked as he resumed his seat.

She shrugged. "I thought I might slip something into your drink, then when you're unconscious I'll ravage your body."

His gaze shot to his coffee cup and he peered at the liquid suspiciously. Serena laughed. "Oh honestly, Gabe, if I ever decide to ravish your body, trust me, I won't want you unconscious."

To her surprise, a deep flush swept over his features. "Your father should have spanked you more often when you were young," he declared.

"My father never spanked me," she protested.

An eyebrow quirked up wryly. "My point exactly."

"Oh, don't be such an old fuddy-duddy," she exclaimed. She stood and walked over to the window. Staring out, she sighed, the long-suffering sigh of a prisoner behind bars seeking elusive freedom.

"Princess, I don't know what you want from me." Gabe's voice was low and controlled. "I can't let you just go off on your own. There could be a kidnapping attempt, or something worse."

She turned to face him. "But only if people know who I am. Your presence makes me obvious. If I was off on my own, nobody would recognize me." She swept her hands toward the window. "There's a sea of humanity out there. I'd just be another tiny little fish.''

"That woman and her daughter recognized you," he countered.

"A mere fluke," Serena replied. She couldn't tell him what she really wanted from him...that she wanted him to love her, to marry her, that she wanted to bear his children and build a life with him.

He'd never once intimated in any way, shape or form that he had any interest in her other than his royal duty. If she confessed this particular fantasy to him, he'd have her back in Wynborough under her parents' wings so fast her head would spin.

If she couldn't have Gabe, then the next best thing was to lose him altogether and see what other men she might meet. Perhaps her fantasies concerning Gabe grew only out of the fact that they spent all their time together. She'd never know the truth of her feelings unless she gained some perspective.

"I see wheels turning," he said, pulling her from her thoughts.

"I was just thinking that it's time to start hunting down Betty Jo Parker. I'll go get her phone number and try to call her." Serena went into her bedroom, her frustration still simmering.

Nobody understood the abiding loneliness that ached inside her. As the youngest of the four sisters, Serena had always felt rather lost in the fracas of her family. She knew her parents loved her dearly, and she was close to all her sisters, but they had to love her—she was family.

Just as so many of the men she dated and the

people in her country loved her because she was a princess. Their affection had nothing to do with real love of the person she was inside, beneath her princess crown.

She opened her purse and grabbed the slip of paper that held the information on Betty Jo Parker, then returned to the main suite.

Gabe had buttoned his shirt and slipped on his jacket, and she was grateful that he now looked less approachable. She was a fool to entertain any kind of fantasies where he was concerned.

"So, remind me where you and your sisters are in this search for Prince James." Gabe said. "I must confess, I haven't kept up on all of it."

Serena sat on the sofa near the telephone. "Well, you know that Beulah Whitaker, who used to work at The Sunshine Home for Children in Arizona, found a baby blanket with the royal emblem on it. That's how we knew it was possible James might be alive and had been adopted."

Gabe nodded. "I also know Katherine went to Albuquerque to see if Trey Sutherland's missing partner, the elusive Bill Lewis, might be Prince James."

"And Bill Lewis has disappeared." And Katherine and Trey had fallen madly in love with each other, Serena thought, wishing the same thing for herself. Lucky Katherine.

She shook away thoughts of her elder sister. "We're hoping that if Betty Jo Parker is Bill's lover, she'll know where he is," Serena explained. She stared down at the slip of paper in her hand. A single phone number and address, it held all the dreams and hopes of finding her brother after all these years. What if it was just another dead end? What if they never found out what really happened to James?

"How did you get the address?" Gabe asked.

Serena flashed him a quick smile. "I pulled a few strings with the phone company. Sometimes it pays to be a princess."

"Why don't we just drive there now?"

Serena frowned, unsure how to explain to Gabe the fear that tore at her heart. She was so afraid of another dead end. She wasn't sure why, but a pre- liminary phone call seemed better than just showing up at the address. "I just think it's better to call first." she finally said.

He nodded as if he'd peeked into her mind and saw her doubts, her fears.

She drew a deep breath and picked up the tele- phone receiver. She punched in the numbers quickly, then sent a small prayer skyward. The phone on the other end of the line rang once... twice...four times, five times. She hung up after it had rung ten times. "There's no answer."

"Try again later. Maybe Betty has a job," Gabe said.

Serena tried all morning to connect with some- body at the phone number she had. Now that she had made the decision to get hold of Betty Jo Parker, it consumed her. She wandered around the suite while Gabe remained at the table reading the paper. When he'd finished reading, he began to work the crossword puzzle.

At noon they ordered room service and after eating Serena continued her phone duty, calling the number every half an hour.

By four, she was going stir-crazy. Gabe had finished the crossword puzzle and was reading a paperback book while she paced back and forth, stopping the agitated walking only to try the number again.

"Maybe we should just drive over there," she finally said. "We could wait around and maybe catch her as she comes home from work."

Gabe nodded. "I'll call for a car."

Within minutes they were on their way to the address Serena had for Betty Jo Parker. As usual, Gabe sat in the front seat with the driver, and Serena sat in the back.

They left the strip and drove into a residential area with houses and yards that were well kept. Serena realized it was easy to think of Las Vegas as a city strictly built for gambling, but in actuality there was a pleasant city beyond the glittering casinos and pawnshops.

They passed a school, the playground empty as all the children were home for the holidays. Greenery and red bows still decorated the lampposts, lingering reminders of the holiday just passed.

In two days it would be New Year's Eve. The way things were shaping up, when the clock struck midnight, Serena would have nobody to kiss. She eyed the back of Gabe's head. Unless she could sneak a kiss from him.

A shiver raced up her spine as she thought of his

lips covering hers. He would be a marvelous kisser, she knew instinctively. His kisses would be firm, commanding...demanding. She sighed. And midnight on New Year's Eve would probably be the first time in months she'd turn around to find him and he'd be nowhere in sight.

She refocused her attention outside the window, noting that the neighborhood they were now in was less attractive, less well kept than the one they had just passed.

Serena sat up straighter in the seat as the driver pulled to the curb in front of a neat white ranch with hunter green shutters.

Gabe turned around. "You want me to go up and knock?"

She shook her head and opened her car door. "I'll do it."

She got out of the car and approached the front door. A wicker rocking chair sat on the porch, as if bidding a visitor to sit and rest a while. A plastic, glittering sign reading Merry Christmas hung on the door.

Serena knocked and waited. As she heard footsteps behind her, she turned to see Gabe approaching. "It doesn't look like anyone's home," he said.

"Maybe she's taking a nap or cooking dinner and didn't hear my knock," Serena replied.

Gabe knocked on the door, his broad knuckles rapping loudly against the wood. "If she's here, she should hear that," he said.

Together they stood...waiting. There was no answer, no noise inside the house to attest to anyone's presence.

Serena sighed in defeat and looked at her watch. "It's nearly five o'clock. Surely if she's at work, she should be home almost anytime."

"Then we'll wait," Gabe said. "We have the driver for as long as we need him."

Serena nodded, and together the two of them started back toward the car. They had almost reached the car when Serena sniffed the air. "I smell charcoal."

"Somebody must be getting ready to barbecue," Gabe replied.

"I think I'll look in the backyard, see if it's Betty," she said. "Maybe that's why she didn't hear us knocking on her door."

"And I'll tell the driver to relax, that we might be here for a while."

As Gabe went toward the car, Serena walked around the side of the house to the back. Almost immediately she saw the next-door neighbor, an older man, placing steaks on his grill and knew that was what she smelled.

There was nobody on Betty's porch. Serena turned to head back to the front of the house, but paused, her gaze roaming beyond Betty's backyard. Houses and sheds everywhere, and not a fence in sight.

She faced the backyard again and took a step forward...then another...and another. Breaking into a run, she had no plan in mind. She only knew opportunity had presented itself, and she intended to grab it with both hands.

She didn't stop running until she was two blocks from Betty Jo Parker's house. Bending over, she breathed deeply in and out, trying to catch her breath.

She'd done it. Her heart did a jump and twirl in joy. She'd managed to lose Gabe. Oh, eventually she'd find him and they would have to go back to Betty's house to find the woman. But for the moment, Serena was free and she intended to savor every second, every minute.

She consciously shoved away images of a very angry Gabe. She'd face her consequences later... after she'd had a little fun.

Still, as she ducked between houses and sheds, the smell of freedom in her nose and the taste of success in her mouth, her mind was clouded with thoughts of a tall, handsome man who just might kill her when she saw him again.

Chapter Four

It only took a couple of minutes of Serena being out of his sight before Gabe got a bad feeling in the pit of his stomach. It was a feeling he'd experienced before...a number of times since being in charge of Serena, and that feeling rarely lied to him.

Telling the driver to stay put, he raced around the side of the house to the backyard.

Nothing. Nobody. Not a single sign of Serena. "Dammit." The epithet exploded from him, startling the man next door, who dropped his spatula and scurried into his house.

Gabe knew better than to yell for her. Even if she were hiding right next to where he stood and he yelled himself hoarse, she wouldn't answer.

He narrowed his eyes, his gaze sweeping the area, seeking a flutter of her scarlet hair, a wisp of teal material from her blouse. Nothing. There was not a sign of Serena anywhere.

He raced back to the car and got in. "Drive very slowly up and down the streets," he said to the astonished driver.

As the car moved at a snail's pace down the street, Gabe continued to look for his princess. Inside he seethed, not only at her, but at himself.

He should have known she would try something. He should have been prepared. But there had been no sign, no subtle signal from her that any such thoughts of escape were in her head.

Still, it was his job to know. It was his job to stay one step ahead of her. "Dammit," he exploded once again, hitting the palm of his hand against the dashboard.

The driver smirked and cast him a sideways glance. "Lovers' quarrel?"

"Something like that," Gabe replied.

"Ah, she'll come back. They always do. And if she doesn't, then you're better off without her."

Terrific, Gabe thought. Not only had he lost the princess, he was now getting romance advice from a man who insisted on wearing his driving hat backward.

"Just keep driving," Gabe replied. "She can't have gotten too far."

Up and down the streets they went, the driver watching the left side and Gabe watching the right, but there was no sign of Serena. It was as if she'd been swallowed by the very street.

It was nearly six-thirty when Gabe directed the driver to take him back to the hotel. Gabe's anger had grown to mammoth proportions, along with his fear, but there was no point in continuing to cruise the streets.

By seven o'clock, he stood in front of the floor-to-ceiling windows in their suite, watching the darkness of night slowly creeping across the sky.

Nighttime in Las Vegas, and Serena was someplace out there alone. His guts twisted at the very thought. Despite her teasing talk, she was such an innocent, easy prey for a smooth-talking operator.

She could be robbed, raped, kidnapped...every heinous crime imaginable played in his mind, filling it with horrifying details of Serena in trouble.

If anything happened to Serena, it would be Gabe's responsibility to tell King Phillip and Queen Gabriella. Gabe clenched his hands into fists and moved away from the window. If anything happened to Serena, he wasn't sure he could handle it.

He eyed the wet bar, knowing a finger of scotch would take off the edge, numb the icy fear that surrounded his heart. He also knew that to succumb to such temptation would be the end of him and his recently realized self-esteem.

It had been his inability to protect another woman that had nearly allowed him to destroy himself three years before. He wouldn't go down that path again...at least not yet.

He jumped as a knock sounded at the door. Hope filled his heart. She was back and didn't have a key. "Serena..." He pulled open the door to find a bellman carrying a huge bouquet of fresh flowers. Like a balloon losing air, the hope seeped out of Gabe.

"Compliments of the management," the young kid said. "Where would you like them?"

"Put them anywhere," he replied irritably.

The kid placed the arrangement in the center of the table, then left.

Alone once again, Gabe sank down on the sofa, knowing his only course of action was to wait…and pray that eventually Serena would return safe and sound.

The hours dragged by. Gabe alternated between pacing and cursing. He stared out the window, then stared at the door. His mind worked overtime to present him with everything horrible that could happen to one beautiful, impulsive, innocent young woman alone on the streets of Las Vegas after dark.

By nine o'clock he could stand his inaction no longer. He left the hotel and began to wander the streets, searching for Serena. In and out of casinos, through dining areas and into nightclubs, Gabe looked everywhere he thought she might be, but with no success.

His anger faded as fear took its place, a relentless fear that tore at his insides. Perhaps he should contact the local authorities? When should he place a call to King Phillip? Where in the hell could Serena be? Damn her and her need to experience life without the burden of her bodyguard.

By midnight, he was once again in their hotel, riding up the elevator to the room. He'd exhausted every possibility and didn't know where else to look for her. There was nothing else he could do but wait for her return…pray for her return.

In the suite, he didn't bother to turn on any lights. The glitter and color of a million lights from nearby casinos and hotels shone into the windows and gave the room a garish illumination.

He sank down on the sofa and closed his eyes. He knew better than anyone that the world was a dangerous place, with too many guns on the streets and too many crazy people in possession of those guns.

Even a simple trip to the local bank on a sunny morning could turn into a journey into death. All it took was one bank robber with an itchy finger.

He shuddered, and tried to push aside images that had haunted him forever. He didn't want to go back there, didn't want to remember that day.

His eyes flicked open as he heard the sound of a key being inserted in the lock of the door. He remained seated as the door opened and Serena entered.

In an instant, relief fluttered through him, intense relief that momentarily made him weak. She appeared safe. Thank God.

In the next instant, that relief dissipated, replaced by an anger so rich, so huge, it filled him to capacity. Serena turned on the lamp near the door, then jumped and yelped in surprise.

"You scared me to death," she exclaimed. "Why were you sitting in the dark? I didn't see you there." She gazed at him for only a moment, then flushed and sat at one of the chairs at the table.

Gabe said nothing. In truth, he was afraid to speak

to her until he reined in the untamed anger that surged inside him.

She kicked off her shoes and massaged one of her feet, still not looking at him.

"What in the hell have you done to your hair?" he asked, suddenly noticing her hair was woven in one long braid down her back, a style he'd never seen her wear before.

She began to knead her other foot. "It was an attempt to remain incognito. I know my hair is sort of my trademark, so I thought if I wore it completely different, it would keep people from recognizing me." She looked up and offered him an uneasy smile. "Do you like it?"

Gabe wondered if the King would forgive him for throttling his youngest daughter. "Do I like it?" He stared at her in amazement. She'd just given him the most miserable night of his life and now she wanted to know if he liked her hairstyle.

He stood, his anger threatening to erupt. "You are truly incredible," he exclaimed. "You run away from me, stay gone for hours, then waltz back in here and want to know if I like your hair?"

In truth, the style was quite becoming, emphasizing her large luminous eyes and the fullness of her mouth. She looked more touchable with her hair in the casual braid, less like a princess and more like a woman he'd love to make love to. The realization only served to further enrage him.

She sat up straight and frowned with a touch of petulance. "Please don't yell at me."

"I can't help it. When I'm angry, I yell," he exclaimed, then drew a deep breath.

"I'd appreciate it if you'd stop," she returned. The petulance faded and excitement lit her features. "Oh, Gabe, I had the most marvelous time tonight." She stood and took a step toward him. "It was just like I'd always dreamed it would be. Nobody knew who I was. I told everyone I met that my name was Sarah Wynn and I was a salesclerk on vacation from Kansas City."

She took two more steps toward him, standing close enough that he could smell the sweet scent of her, see the tiny golden flecks that mingled with the green of her eyes. She placed a hand on his arm. "I met a wonderful man, and he took me out to dinner, then we danced the night away. His name is Avery Kintell and he's an investment banker from here in Las Vegas."

She'd met a man. A wonderful man. The words reverberated through Gabe's head, serving to stoke the fires of his rage even higher.

He jerked away from her touch. "How nice for you," he said sarcastically. "And while you were dining and dancing the night away, I was back here trying to figure out how to tell your mother and father that they'd lost another child." He didn't mince words. "I didn't know if you'd been kidnapped, or worse."

The light in her eyes dimmed. "I'm sorry, Gabe. I didn't mean to worry you."

"Didn't mean to worry me?" The words exploded from him, his anger unleashed and wild.

"When exactly did you not mean to worry me? While I was driving up and down the streets, wondering where you'd gone, what had happened to you? Or perhaps later, when it got dark and I went into every casino, every restaurant and nightclub in a ten-block radius, searching for you?"

"You're yelling again," she said, her voice tiny compared to his.

"Hell yes, I'm yelling." The words roared out of him. "You need to be yelled at. You don't have the luxury of forgetting who you are...what you are. You're a princess, and because of that you're always at risk."

"I was fine tonight," she countered with a touch of defiance.

"You were damned lucky tonight," he replied. "It only takes one nut, Serena. One crazy person out to prove a point or looking for a king's ransom. What you did tonight was selfish, and self-indulgent, without regard for me, or your parents, or your country."

Tears welled up in her eyes. "I said I was sorry. I won't do it again, okay?"

Gabe wanted to take her in his arms, kiss away the tears his words had created, and the impulse only made him angry all over again. "You're spoiled, Serena. Spoiled and willful, and someday those two traits are going to get you in a world of trouble."

He barely got the words out of his mouth when she turned from him and ran to her room. He fought his desire to run after her, to somehow ease the hurt he'd inflicted.

She needed to think about what he'd said, needed to understand that no matter how badly she wanted to be just a normal, average young woman, she couldn't be.

He sat back down on the sofa and drew a deep breath. At least she was home, safe and sound. All the horrendous scenarios for disaster that had crossed his mind had not come true.

He should be feeling enormous relief, but instead a wave of impending doom swept through him. And he suspected the cause of it was that she'd met a man...a wonderful man.

Serena found her bed through a veil of tears and threw herself across it. Her tears burned hot as sobs escaped from her.

Gabriel Morgan was the meanest, most hateful man she'd ever known. His words burned in her brain. Spoiled. Willful. Selfish and self-indulgent. How could he be so cruel? To say such hateful, hurtful things to her. Was that what he really believed about her?

The thought that he believed her to be such horrid things only served to make her cry harder. She wanted Gabe to like her. She wanted that more than anything in the world.

It took only a few minutes for her tears to be spent. When she was finished crying, she sat up and swiped the last of her tears with her fingers.

She wanted to hate Gabe for all the things he'd said, but in her heart, she knew there was more than a little truth in those words.

She hadn't given much thought to consequences when she'd taken flight from Gabe. Oh, she'd known she would face his ire when she returned, but she hadn't considered all the dire things that might have happened to her.

As she imagined Gabe having to call her mother and father to tell them she'd been kidnapped or worse, her heart constricted. Her parents had learned to live with James's disappearance, had coped with the realization that they'd never see their only son again. But losing another child would be devastating, and Serena would never want to be responsible for hurting her parents in any way.

Swiping her hair from her face, she remembered the way Gabe had looked when she'd turned on the light. His face had been drawn and pale, his hair askew as if he'd run his hands through it a hundred times. He'd looked like a man who'd worried himself half to death. Shame coursed through her.

Gabe was right. She'd been willful and self-indulgent. And as much as she'd like to be normal and average, she would never be anything but a princess and there were certain responsibilities that came along with her birthright.

As much as she hated to admit it, she owed Gabe a huge apology, and a promise that she would never, ever again sneak away from him and go off on her own.

With this thought in mind, she opened the door to her room and peered out into the darkened suite. The curtains had been pulled over the windows and she assumed Gabe had gone to bed in his room.

She crept across the floor of the main area to Gabe's bedroom door. No glimmer of light shone beneath the door. For a moment irritation swept through her, irritation that he could say such mean things, then just go to sleep so easily. She shoved away the irritation, not wanting it to get in the way of her apology and knocked on the door.

"What do you want?"

His voice came from behind her, startling her. She jumped and whirled around. "Where are you?" she asked, narrowing her eyes in an attempt to penetrate the darkness of the room.

The lamp next to the sofa lit. Gabe was stretched out on the sofa, a blanket covering him from the waist down. He was bare chested and as Serena stared at his broad, muscled chest, she momentarily forgot why she'd sought him out in the first place.

She'd never seen him in anything other than his official uniform, the navy suit and white shirt. She'd certainly never seen him half-naked before.

Dark hair dusted the center of his chest and Serena's fingers itched to dance in that hair and feel the warmth of his skin beneath.

"Princess?"

His voice broke her momentary inertia and she flushed with the heat of her thoughts. "What are you doing out here?" she asked.

"What do you think?" he returned, an edge in his voice. "You snuck away from me once, but it won't happen again." He sat up, his dark gaze intense. "You won't get away from me a second time. I'm going to be on you like tread on a tire, Serena."

"That's what I came out to tell you." She averted her gaze from him, unable to think with the distraction of his bare chest. "Everything you said before was true. I have been selfish and self-absorbed, and tonight I took a risk that I shouldn't have."

She paused a moment and snuck a quick glance at him. His facial features radiated cynicism. "I mean it, Gabe. There's no reason for you to sleep out here with one eye open. You won't have to worry about me trying to get away from you again. I promise I won't."

"You'll make my job a lot easier with your full cooperation," he finally said.

"I know." She frowned. "Avery has invited me out tomorrow night and I intend to go, but I don't intend to tell him who I really am." She ignored Gabe's frown. "He thinks I'm Sarah Wynn from Kansas City and I want it to stay that way."

"So how do you intend to explain Sarah Wynn having a bodyguard?" he asked.

"We'll tell him that you're an old family friend, and you couldn't find a date so I invited you to tag along with us." She held up her hands as his frown deepened. "I know it's not a perfect solution, but it will work for the short-term."

He hesitated a moment, then nodded. "If that's what you wish."

"It is," Serena replied. She paused a moment, drinking in the vision he made with his bare chest and slightly mussed hair. What she really wished was that she could curl up on the sofa next to him, feel that beautiful broad chest against her own, be embraced by him and held through the night.

"Was there something else?" he asked.

Again, a flush swept over Serena's face, warming her cheeks. "One more thing. In the morning I'd like to go back by Betty Jo Parker's house. If she isn't home again, maybe we could talk to the neighbors, ask them when she is normally home."

"Okay," Gabe said.

"Well...I guess this is good-night," she said. There was nothing else to say to him. She'd apologized and she'd promised never again to try to escape from him. What she wanted to do was beg him not to think badly of her, ask him to take back the things he'd said. Instead, she went back into her bedroom and closed the door.

As she put on her nightgown and got into bed, she shoved away thoughts of the man who was paid to be with her, a man who'd never given any indication that she was anything but a duty, and instead thought of Avery Kintell.

When Serena had lost Gabe in Betty Jo Parker's neighborhood, she'd figured she would have to walk back to the strip. She'd run without her purse, without money so she couldn't catch a bus or a cab.

She'd lucked out when a little old woman in a luxury car had pulled up beside her and offered her a ride.

"I normally don't pick up hitchhikers," the old woman had said as she'd motioned Serena into the car. "But you look a little down and out."

"My boyfriend and I had a fight," Serena said,

the lie tasting bad in her mouth. "I took off without thinking and didn't grab my purse or anything."

The old woman had smiled and winked at Serena. "Lovers' spats. They're all the same...mostly a waste of time. Make love, not war, that's what I say."

She'd dropped Serena in front of the Flamingo Casino. The Flamingo was far enough away from her hotel that Serena was fairly certain she wouldn't run into Gabe. In the lobby of the Flamingo the management was offering free hors d'oeuvres and cocktails. Serena had been sampling a couple of tiny egg rolls when Avery had approached her.

He was attractive, although not nearly as handsome as Gabe. But he'd gazed at Serena as if she were one of the wonders of the world. As they'd gotten to know each other, he'd hung on her every word, devoting his full attention to her. It had been a heady experience for Serena.

From the Flamingo, they had gone to dinner at a nice Italian place, then gone dancing at an upscale club. All in all, it had been the kind of normal dating evening that Serena had never experienced.

When Avery had kissed her good-night at the end of their evening together, there had been no bells or whistles. It had been pleasant, but not earth-shattering.

Serena supposed first kisses were never particularly earth-shattering. It took time for passion to grow, time for bells and whistles to resound from a kiss.

She closed her eyes, trying to summon a visual

picture of Avery in her mind. She'd liked him...and it had been obvious he was crazy about her. And he had no idea she was anything but a salesclerk from Kansas City.

What she couldn't understand was why her mind refused to produce his image? Why was her head so filled with visions of a dark-haired, dark-eyed man, bare chested on a sofa?

Chapter Five

"I see she came back," the driver said, smirking the next afternoon as Gabe and Serena got into the car for a second trip to Betty Jo Parker's house. "Told you she would." He shook his head and grinned. "Women...we can't live without them."

"Yeah, you're a romantic genius," Gabe replied dryly.

Though a quiet understanding existed between Gabe and Serena now, the air had been tense as they had shared morning coffee, then an early lunch.

After she had gone back to her room the night before, Gabe had left the sofa and gone into his bedroom. Despite the fact that he knew Serena to be willful and impulsive, spoiled and spirited, he also knew she was a young woman of honor. She had given him her promise that she wouldn't try to lose him again, and he knew no matter how great the temptation, she would adhere to that promise.

He'd climbed into the crisp, clean sheets of the king-size bed, anticipating the first good night's sleep in months. But instead of a good night's sleep, his slumber had been disturbed by dreams...dreams of Serena.

In those dreams, her hair had been braided, and he'd slowly unwound it, the silky strands sensually soft against his fingers. And the unwinding of those locks of hair had only been the beginning in a ritual of lovemaking.

With her hair loose and flowing down her back, they had shared a kiss...a kiss that seared his lips with heat and created a raging fire in his veins.

When the kiss ended, she'd stood in front of him and slowly undressed, sliding off the teal blouse to display a wispy white bra that increased the inferno inside him. When the blouse fell to the floor, she unclasped her bra, exposing perfect breasts. Her slacks followed the blouse and bra, leaving her clad only in a pair of silky panties.

With desire surging inside him, he'd reached for her and pulled her down on the bed with him. Again they kissed, her lips the sweet honey he'd always known they would be.

And that was when the dream had changed. Suddenly he was sitting on a chair in the corner and another man was in the bed with Serena. He knew the man was Avery Kintell and at that moment Gabe had awakened, filled with jealousy and yearning with desire for the flame-haired woman.

The unsettling quality of the dream had stayed with him throughout the early morning. As he'd sat across from Serena at the table, he'd tried to shove it aside, telling himself that dreams were nothing more than crazy sleep images and meant nothing whatsoever.

Just because he'd dreamed that Serena was making love to Avery, didn't mean it was going to happen. He would make sure it didn't happen. He wasn't about to let her first love experience be with a man who had picked her up in a casino lobby. But in any case, the bottom line was that it really was none of his business.

"I hope she's home today," Serena said from the back seat of the car, pulling Gabe from his disturbing thoughts. "I really want to get this resolved."

"One way or another, we'll get some information," Gabe assured her. The man who had been barbecuing the day before had looked old enough to be retired. Even if Betty wasn't home, Gabe hoped the neighbor would be and would know Betty's work hours.

Within minutes the car was once again parked at the curb in front of the neat little house. Together, Serena and Gabe walked up to the door. Gabe knocked and they waited.

"The curtains are all drawn and it doesn't look like anyone is home," Serena said with a touch of disappointment.

Gabe knocked again. They waited for a reply and when none was forthcoming, he nodded toward the house next door. "Let's see if the neighbor knows when she might be home."

They left Betty's porch and went to the house

next door, where Gabe's knock was answered by the elderly man who'd been cooking outside the day before.

"Hi, we've been trying to get hold of Betty Jo Parker from next door," Serena said. "But we're having problems catching her at home."

"Course you are," the man replied. "Betty don't live there anymore. She moved a couple days ago."

"Oh no!" Serena exclaimed. "She can't be gone." Serena's voice held a heavy layer of disappointment.

"Do you know where she moved to?" Gabe asked.

"'Fraid not." The old man scratched his head thoughtfully. "Although she did mention a sweet little apartment she'd found on the north side of town."

"But she didn't say anything more specific?" Gabe pressed.

"Think. Surely she said something about her new address...something that would let you know more about where she was moving," Serena said with a touch of desperation.

"Nah, Betty wasn't one of those women who felt the need to spill her guts about her personal life." He shrugged. "Sorry I can't be of more help."

"Thank you, anyway," Gabe replied. Serena nodded, as if too disheartened to speak.

The old man started to close the door, then re-opened it. "If it helps at all, last I heard Betty was working down at Harrah's Casino. Maybe you can catch her there."

Serena's face lit with excitement and a responding rush of desire swept through Gabe. When she looked the way she did at that moment, her eyes all shiny and bright, happiness lighting her up from within, she was incredibly magnetic. A man would have to be completely dead inside not to feel some response to her.

As he followed her back to the car, he accepted the fact that he wanted Serena. He wanted her in his arms, in his bed. He wanted to be the man who introduced her to physical pleasure, the man who'd watch her eyes as they darkened with abandonment.

Along with the acknowledgment of his desire for her came the knowledge that he'd never have her. Another man would experience the pleasure of initiating her in the art of lovemaking.

It was right that it would be another man. She deserved that her first time making love be with a man who loved her. And Gabe would never love her, or anyone else. His heart was completely closed, unavailable to the emotion of love.

They went directly to Harrah's, where the personnel manager told them that Betty was no longer with them, although the manager said he thought Betty had gone to work at another casino, but he couldn't remember which one.

"Maybe I can call the local authorities and see if they can hunt down this Betty Jo Parker," Gabe suggested when they were back in their hotel room.

"Oh, Gabe, that would be wonderful," Serena exclaimed. "Do you really think they'll help us?"

He smiled at her in genuine amusement. She was

truly an innocent when it came to recognizing the power of her position. Despite the fact that in the United States she had no real power or position, he didn't think the Las Vegas police department would alienate a visiting princess. "I'm sure they'll bend over backward to help you as long as we explain the situation."

It took only minutes for Gabe to make the phone call. He got in touch with a Lieutenant Breckenridge and explained who he was and what they needed. Breckenridge was hesitant at first, but finally agreed to do what he could to help them in their search for Betty Jo Parker. It didn't hurt when Gabe mentioned his own background as one of the boys in blue.

As Gabe hung up the phone, a knock sounded at the door. Gabe answered, surprised to see the bellman with yet another bouquet of flowers, this time a dozen long-stem yellow roses. "The gentleman said to send these here for a Sarah Wynn?" He looked at Gabe, then at Serena, who clapped her hands together with excitement.

"Thank you, I'll take them," she said. She took the bouquet and set them on the coffee table. She sat down on the sofa, then withdrew the card that was stuck amid the blooms.

Gabe tipped the bellman, then turned in time to see Serena read the card, a blush sweeping over her features. "Oh, isn't that sweet," she murmured, more to herself than to him.

"I assume they're from Mr. Wonderful," Gabe observed, trying to keep any sarcasm from his voice, but having a hard time.

"Yes...from Avery," she replied. She jumped up, the card clutched to her breast. "He's going to pick me up at five." She looked at her watch. "I think I'll go take a nice, long bubble bath."

She nearly floated from the room, humming a lilting melody as she closed her bedroom door.

Gabe eyed the roses with distaste. How boring. How utterly predictable. Everyone sent roses. If he were going to send Serena flowers, he'd choose something wild and vivid, an exotic bloom as unique and vibrant as her.

He frowned, unsure if the disgust he felt was for the flowers, the man who had sent them, or himself for spending a mere second contemplating what kind of flowers he'd send Serena.

While Serena was taking a nice, long, hot bubble bath to prepare for the evening, Gabe thought perhaps he better take a bracing, cold shower. If he was going to spend the evening as a third wheel with Serena and Mr. Rosebud, he had a feeling it was going to be a trying, difficult night.

Two hours later, he sat with Avery Kintell and Serena at a table in a Chinese restaurant, listening to Avery tell Serena what it had been like for him to grow up in Vegas.

As she had planned, Serena introduced Avery to Gabe as an old family friend and explained that Gabe would be accompanying them that evening. Although Gabe had seen a swift flicker of disappointment in Avery's pale blue eyes, it had quickly been hidden beneath a pleasant smile and a welcoming handshake.

The man talked as though he had money. His chest puffed out each time he spoke of his success as an investment banker, and yet something didn't ring true about him. He wore an expensive suit, but the shirt beneath was frayed around the collar. Gabe had noticed his shoes, although shined to a high gloss, were old and worn.

Serena, on the other hand, looked more lovely than Gabe had ever seen her. Clad in a coral-colored silk dress and with her hair pulled up off her neck and twisted in an intricate fashion, she looked elegant, yet strangely vulnerable.

Dinner was relatively pleasant, with Serena and Avery talking about places they'd visited and places they would like to go. Gabe knew Serena was consciously studying every word she said, not wanting to ruin the image she'd created of herself as a salesclerk from Kansas City.

Gabe listened carefully to everything Avery said, still unsettled by a bad feeling where the man was concerned. He wasn't sure if it was specifically Avery or if he'd feel the same way about any man Serena appeared interested in.

"That store you work at back in Kansas City must pay you quite well," Avery observed when they'd finished eating.

"Why do you say that?" Serena asked.

"When I dropped you at your door last night, I couldn't help but notice you were staying in the penthouse," Avery explained.

"Oh...that..." Serena stuttered and Gabe could

see the wheels turning in her head as she sought a logical explanation.

"Gabe got the room," she finally said. "He has loads of money. His family is quite wealthy."

Gabe frowned at her, not approving of the web of lies she was spinning.

Avery looked at Gabe. "I was wondering what you did for a living."

Gabe shrugged. "A little bit of this and a little bit of that." He sensed Serena's audible sigh of relief at his answer. He supposed there was no real harm in playing her game for an evening.

"I couldn't help but notice the crest on your jacket," Avery said.

"Uh...my family crest," Gabe replied.

Gabe was relieved when dinner was over and the three of them left the restaurant. He didn't like Avery Kintell, and he wasn't sure why. All he knew was that the man gave him a bad feeling. Avery was smooth as butter, but Gabe sensed a slimy side that was disturbing.

From the restaurant, they went to a club, where the dance floor was huge, the music loud, and despite the early hour a large crowd had already gathered.

Serena and Avery settled at a table next to the bar, and Gabe took up residency on one of the stools at the bar. From his vantage point he was close enough to guard Serena, yet give her a little privacy with Kintell.

"Hi, handsome." The bartender, an attractive buxom blond, smiled at him. Her blue eyes gleamed flirtatiously as she leaned over the bar toward him. "What can I get for you?"

"Just a cola," he replied, then twirled his stool around so he had a perfect view of Serena's table and the dance floor.

As he sipped his drink, he watched Avery and Serena. He didn't like the way the man touched her so often, a hand on her hand, an arm around her shoulder, a touch to her cheek. They were light, casual touches intended to promote familiarity...intimacy.

"Here you are." The bartender placed his drink in front of him.

"Thanks." Gabe flashed her a quick smile.

"Big crowd tonight," she said and pointed to the dance floor. "Guess everyone is practicing partying for tomorrow night."

"Tomorrow night?" Gabe looked at her curiously.

"New Year's Eve."

"Oh yeah, that's right. It is tomorrow night, isn't it?" Somehow Gabe had managed to lose track of the holidays. Christmas had been a quiet day.

He took a sip of his soda, his mind whirling back to Christmas morning. Serena had awakened early and he'd found her sitting next to the Christmas tree. He'd known by the look on her face that she was missing her family.

Even solemn, she'd been beautiful. She'd worn an emerald robe and her hair had been sleep-tousled. As he handed her the small gift he'd bought for her, he'd wanted to wrap her in his arms and carry her to his bed.

She'd opened the present, exclaiming over the variety of scented soaps and bath oils. Gabe's mind had worked overtime, presenting him with an image of her in the bathtub, surrounded by bubbles, her body slick with sweet-smelling oil.

She'd surprised him with a gift, a leather shaving kit to replace the battered, torn one he normally used. He vividly remembered the pleasure she'd shown when he promised to use it every day.

For the remainder of the day, Gabe had fought a growing awareness of Serena not as a princess, but as a woman...a desirable, beautiful woman.

"So, are you alone or with somebody?" The bartender's question pulled him from his thoughts.

"I'm sort of with friends." He pointed to Avery and Serena's table.

"You're with Avery?" There was a distinct coolness in her voice.

Gabe looked at her. "You know him?"

She snorted indelicately. "Everyone knows Avery."

"Actually, I've only just met the man tonight. I'm friends with the lady he's with," Gabe explained.

The woman looked at Serena and shook her head with a knowing smile. "She's not his usual type. Normally Avery likes them very old, very ill and very wealthy."

Every muscle in Gabe's body tensed. "He's a con man?" he asked.

The blonde laughed. "Avery wrote the book on

con.'' She grabbed a damp cloth and swiped the top of the bar. ''If your lady friend has money, if you care about her at all, you'll warn her that Avery will wine and dine her right out of her fortune. He'll marry her, then leave her broke and broken. That's what he does for a living. Oh yeah, Avery is always looking to score.''

''Looking to score.'' The words echoed loudly in Gabe's head. Looking to score with a princess...Gabe's princess. Not in this lifetime, he vowed.

''He doesn't exactly look real prosperous,'' Gabe observed.

''Avery is good at getting money. He just isn't very smart about keeping it. The man has a major gambling problem and that's what keeps him constantly on the prowl.''

On the prowl. Gabe fought his impulse to rush over to Serena, throw her over his shoulder and carry her as far away from Kintell as possible. He knew as long as he kept her in his sight, nothing was going to happen to her.

He frowned thoughtfully. Poor Serena. She'd been so happy, so certain that her appeal to Avery Kintell was genuine, that he had no clue she was anything but a salesclerk.

Gabe would bet his sanity that Avery Kintell knew exactly who and what Serena was. Like the woman with her little girl the day before, Avery had known the minute he'd seen Serena that she was a Princess of Wynborough.

Damn him. Damn the man for putting Gabe in an

untenable position. As he watched Serena laugh at something Kintell said, Gabe's heart ached for her.

Gabe knew he had two choices: allow her to continue to see Avery for the remainder of their stay in Las Vegas and hope she didn't do anything foolish, or tell her the truth about the man and break her heart into a thousand pieces. At the moment, neither choice seemed the right one.

Serena wasn't having as good a time as she'd thought she would. Although Avery was as attentive, as wonderful as he'd been the night before, the excitement of the previous night was gone. She wondered if part of the fun of last night had been because she'd successfully snuck away from Gabe.

Gabe. Part of the problem was that his very presence distracted her from Avery. When Avery touched her hand, she wished it were Gabe's touch she felt. As Avery gazed into her eyes, she wished it were dark brown ones looking at her with such adoration.

Drat the man for confusing her so. She looked over to where he sat talking to the striking blond bartender. She frowned. What was he doing? What were they talking about? The woman wore a blouse cut so low her ample breasts were on display, and Gabe certainly didn't seem to mind the exhibition.

Emotion, rich and deep, flooded through her, an emotion she recognized as pure, unadulterated jealousy. It surprised her…and irritated her.

How could Gabe protect her if he had all his attention focused on the blond babe? Avery could throttle me right here and now and Gabe wouldn't even notice, she thought indignantly.

She knew she was being silly. Avery wasn't about to choke her, and if he did, Gabe would put the man to the floor before Serena could blink her eyes. Gabe might be enjoying the company of the bosomy bartender, but Serena knew that didn't mean he wasn't keeping a close watch on her. He was good at his job. Serena couldn't fault him there.

"Come on, Avery. Let's dance," she said.

She led Avery onto the dance floor, fighting for space amid the sea of gyrating couples. She and Avery had only begun to dance when Gabe and the tall blonde appeared next to them. Apparently the bartender was on break and had decided to spend part of her free time dancing with Gabe.

Serena had never seen Gabe dance before, and she was unsurprised to discover that despite his brawn, he was graceful and light on his feet. He flashed her a smile and her heart stepped up its rhythm.

She studiously ignored him and tried to do so for the remainder of the night. It was in the wee hours of the early morning when Gabe and Serena returned to their hotel suite.

Serena immediately went to bed, exhausted not only by the hours of dancing, but also by the knowledge that she had a wonderful man half-crazy for her, and a fixation on another man who she wasn't even sure liked her most of the time.

Thankfully, her sleep was dreamless and restful. She awakened at noon, to the scent of something delicious filling the air. She showered and dressed quickly, her stomach rumbling with hunger pangs.

"Something smells marvelous," she said as she left her room.

"Chicken Kiev," Gabe said. He pointed to the chair opposite him at the table, where a covered plate awaited her. "I wasn't sure what time you'd be awake, but I got hungry so I went ahead and ordered."

"I'm starving," she said. She sat and uncovered the dish and dug in. They ate in silence, and as the silence lingered, Serena sensed tension radiating from Gabe.

"Anything wrong?" she asked.

He hesitated a moment, then shook his head. "No, everything is fine."

But she sensed something bothering him. Whatever it was, it kept him quiet and introspective for the day. They spent the afternoon in stifling silence, waiting for the phone to ring, waiting for Lieutenant Breckenridge to call and tell them what he'd discovered about Betty Jo Parker's whereabouts.

The only interruption to their silence came when the bellman knocked, once again bearing roses from Avery. She read the note that came along with the flowers, then looked at Gabe.

"Avery has invited me to the New Year's Eve party here in the hotel ballroom this evening," she said. She eyed Gabe to see his reaction. "Dinner and cocktails begin at six. He says he's planned an extra special evening, one with the possibility to change my life. Maybe he intends to propose to me.''

"That's ridiculous. You hardly know the man," Gabe scoffed. A small tic pulsed in his jaw.

"Sometimes you meet somebody and within hours you know that's the person you'd like to spend the rest of your life with.'' Serena wasn't sure why she said this; she certainly wasn't in love with Avery Kintell, although she enjoyed his company.

"The man isn't right for you," Gabe said, the tic in his jaw more pronounced.

"You can't know that," she protested. "He's nice, and he's sweet. He looks at me like nobody ever has before. And best of all, he likes *me*, not Princess Serena Wyndham of Wynborough.''

Gabe stared at her for a long moment, then turned away. "If he's picking you up at six, hadn't you better start getting ready?''

"Yes, I suppose I should," Serena agreed. She frowned as she went into her bedroom, certain that Gabe had something on his mind...something weighty. But unless he decided to share it with her, there was nothing she could do about it.

She wasn't sure why she'd told Gabe that Avery might propose this evening, although a proposal from him wouldn't surprise her. He'd spent the night before talking about how well matched they were and extolling the virtues of marriage and life in Las Vegas.

Although she had no intention of accepting a proposal, she'd wanted to see what Gabe's reaction would be to such a possibility. His reaction had been decidedly underwhelming. Just that tic in his jaw...and she didn't know exactly what that signi-fied.

At least tonight, when the clock struck midnight to ring in a new year, she'd have somebody to kiss her. She studiously refused to consider that the one man she most wanted to kiss her wouldn't.

She dressed with care, determined to have a good time no matter how taciturn, how moody Gabe remained. The outfit she chose to wear was a winter-white two-piece suit, the material shot through with strands of gold thread.

Once dressed, she eyed herself in the mirror with satisfaction. The tailored suit jacket hugged her curves, the deep neckline displaying just the right amount of cleavage. She looked festive and ready for a night of fun.

It was a quarter to five when she left her room. Gabe stood as she entered, his gaze dark and brood-ing as it raked over her from head to toe. The tic in his jaw was more pronounced than she'd ever seen.

"Get your purse," he said. "I've got the driver waiting."

"The driver? I don't understand. Avery will be here in just a few minutes."

"Avery will be here and you won't." He took her by the arm and propelled her toward the door.

"Gabe..." she sputtered in protest, wondering if he'd lost his mind, if somehow she'd managed to push him over the edge into insanity.

"Just don't say anything," he demanded, and

something about the look in his eyes warned her to keep her mouth shut.

She managed to stay quiet until he escorted her into the back of the awaiting car and he got in the front seat.

"Take us to Ye Olde Wedding Chapel," he instructed the driver.

"Would you please tell me what's going on?" she asked. "Why on earth are we going to Ye Olde Wedding Chapel?"

He turned in the seat and looked at her with a tight smile. "Why else would we be going there? We're going to the chapel and we're going to get married."

Chapter Six

"Whewee, sounds like that old song," the driver exclaimed. "You know, that one about going to the chapel of love…what was the name of that group that sang that song…one of them girl groups."

Gabe ignored the man and remained focused on Serena.

"We're getting married?" Her face radiated myriad emotions…confusion, bewilderment…and something else that Gabe refused to consider, something that looked amazingly like excitement.

"Hot damn," the driver exclaimed with a hoot of enthusiasm. "I knew the two of you were meant for each other the moment I laid eyes on you. Darned if I don't feel like Cupid."

"Just drive," Gabe demanded.

He wondered if his pronouncement had caused some sort of shock in Serena. He'd expected her to kick and buck, throw one of her royal fits, but she didn't say a word as they drove the short distance to the chapel.

Gabe knew he was definitely experiencing some sort of crazy shock. When she'd walked out of her bedroom in the white suit, with her hair all loose and curly and her cheeks flushed with color, he'd made an instant decision. She looked like a bride…he'd make her one.

If he married her, he'd keep her safe from Avery Kintell and every other man she might meet while in Las Vegas, and he'd never have to tell her the truth about Kintell and break her heart. He steadfastly refused to consider his king and queen's reaction to his marrying their youngest daughter. He'd face that hailstorm when it happened.

It was a desperate scheme to prevent dire circumstances. But Gabe knew one thing. If Serena was married to him, she wouldn't be available for any fortune hunters or a quick roll in the hay by a smooth-talking operator. And Avery Kintell was definitely bad news. A quick call to Lieutenant Breckenridge had confirmed that the man was trouble with a capital *T*. Gabe had to do something…and fast.

When the driver pulled up to the curb in front of Ye Olde Wedding Chapel, Gabe told him to wait, then he and Serena went inside the building.

She was more subdued than he'd ever seen her. He'd expected a royal protest of his plan, but as they stepped into the lobby, she simply looked up at him and smiled shyly. "Can I have a bouquet?" she asked.

The request, so simply, so sweetly asked, touched Gabe. Before he could answer her, the minister of the chapel greeted them.

"Welcome," he said and held out a hand to Gabe. "I'm Edward Doyle, minister of this church."

"I'm Gabriel Morgan and this is Serena Wyndham. We'd like to get married," Gabe blurted. He felt a sudden urgency to get this over and done with before he changed his mind.

On the one hand, he knew it was the most logical answer to the problem of safeguarding Serena. On the other hand, his nerves jumped and jittered in protest of what they were about to do. It felt too real, and he didn't intend for it to be real.

"Wonderful," Edward exclaimed, beaming at both of them. "There is nothing I enjoy more than uniting two people in love."

Gabe bit back his protest. He wanted to confess that he didn't love Serena, that this marriage ceremony had nothing to do with love. "Uh...we need flowers," he said instead. "And we don't have rings."

Edward nodded, his bulbous nose appearing to grow red with joy. "We provide everything you need for an occasion to remember." He turned to Serena and gestured to the flower case. "What kind of flowers would the bride like to carry?"

Serena appeared to be in a daze. Her eyes were more lustrous than Gabe had ever seen them, and her hand trembled slightly as she pointed to a lovely bouquet of orchids with a trailing ribbon of pale lavender.

A momentary thrill rushed through Gabe as he realized she'd eschewed the rose bouquets in favor of the exotic orchids. He'd been right and Avery had been wrong. She was more than a rose kind of woman.

"Wonderful," Edward exclaimed as he handed her the bouquet. "And now if the two of you would step into my office, we'll make the necessary arrangements and I have a variety of rings for you to choose from."

The next few minutes passed in a haze for Gabe. They chose the kind of ceremony they wanted, then he picked out a gold band for her. She surprised him by insisting that he get a gold band for himself as well.

All too quickly he and Serena stood before the simple altar, listening to Edward Doyle speak of love through eternity and cleaving unto one another. Gabe felt as if he'd stepped into a dream.

Serena looked every inch a true bride in her white suit. The scent of the orchids filled the air, mingling with her perfume and dizzying Gabe's senses.

Nothing seemed quite real as he faced Serena, repeated the vows of a man to a woman, and slipped the gold band onto her finger.

As she echoed those vows, her voice quivered and her eyes filled with tears. She looked so lovely, so vulnerable, and Gabe had a feeling he was making the biggest mistake of his life. He should have explained to her what he intended with the marriage. He should have told her the rules before they came to this place in time.

It was too late now. He'd have to explain after the ceremony. He needed to explain to her that it wasn't a real marriage. Oh, it was legal, but it would never be binding. He'd see to that. But at the moment it was difficult to think about rules or about good intentions; it was difficult to focus on anything but Serena's loveliness and the luminous shine of her eyes.

"I now pronounce you husband and wife." The minister's words pulled Gabe back from his thoughts. "You may kiss your bride."

Kiss your bride. Gabe looked at Serena. Her lips were parted as if in eagerness, and the last thing he wanted to do was to kiss her...because what he wanted to do most of all was to kiss her.

He leaned forward, intending a circumspect little peck on her mouth, but she apparently had other designs. With tears streaming down her cheeks, she wrapped her arms around his neck and pressed her body into his.

He didn't have a chance to protest, and in any case, whatever protest that might have flown through his mind was lost as her lips met his.

Sweeter than he'd ever imagined, softer than he'd ever fantasized, her mouth plied his with heat, and for a moment he was lost to the heady pleasure of kissing Serena.

When the kiss finally ended, Gabe stepped away from her, needing to distance himself from the beckoning invitation that remained in her gaze.

He took her by the arm. "Come on, let's get out of here."

She said nothing until they were out on the sidewalk next to the car. "Gabe?" There was a soft yearning in her eyes, a need to understand what they had just done.

Despite his reluctance to touch her, he grazed a finger down her cheek. "We'll talk later, in the privacy of our room," he said.

She nodded, apparently satisfied for the moment. When they got back to the hotel, the New Year's Eve celebration was in full swing, revelers spilling out of the ballroom and into the lobby.

"Let's join the celebration," Gabe suggested. He was eager to find Avery Kintell and see the man's face when he realized his attempted scam had been ruined.

"Okay," she agreed with little enthusiasm. Obviously she'd hoped for a more private celebration, but that was exactly what Gabe intended to avoid.

He couldn't tell what she thought about their sudden marriage, but he knew instinctively what he had to tell her later would probably make her angry...or make her cry. He dreaded doing either, but he could stand her anger far easier than he could stand her tears. Better to put it all off for as long as possible.

The live band was loud, the dance floor already packed, as they made their way through the crowd. They found an empty table, complete with party hats and confetti. Appropriately, the two hats on their table were a cardboard tiara and a top hat. Serena placed the tiara on her head as she ordered a bottle of champagne from the waiter.

The tiara, although flimsy and garish, sparkled

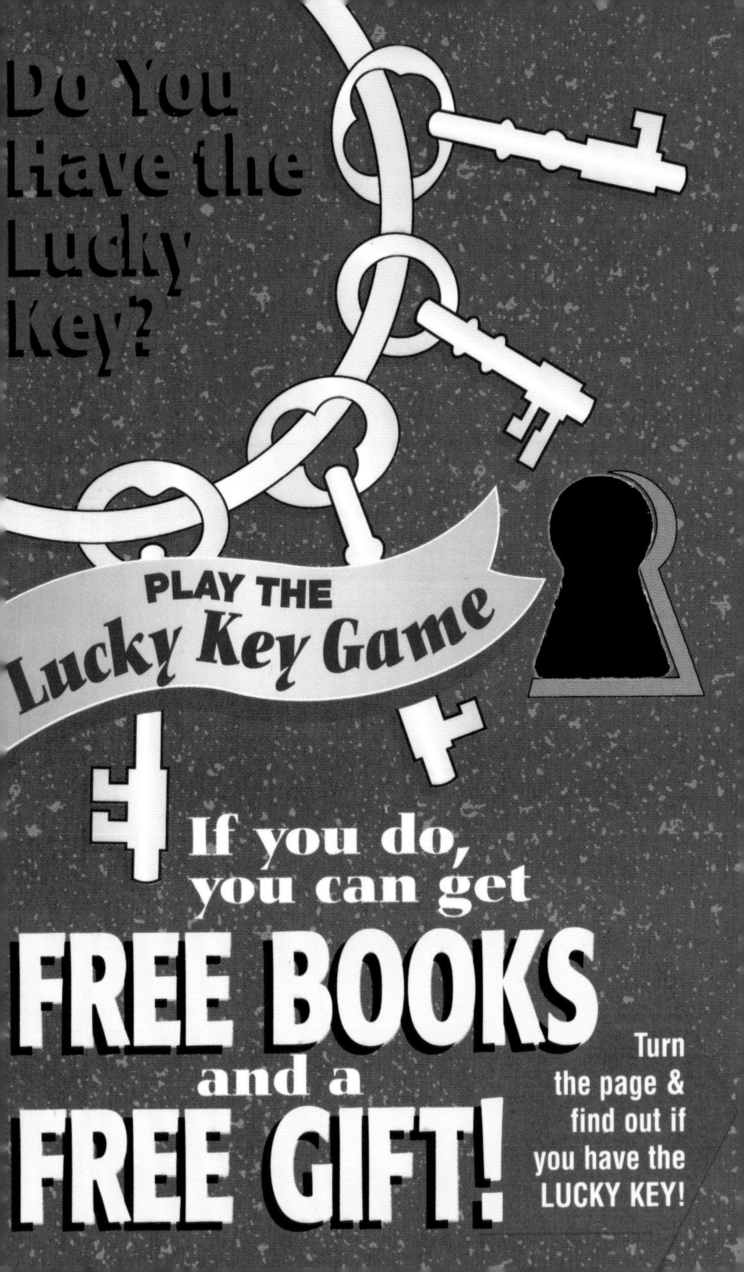
Do You Have the Lucky Key?
PLAY THE
Lucky Key Game
If you do, you can get
FREE BOOKS
and a
FREE GIFT!
Turn the page & find out if you have the LUCKY KEY!

PLAY THE
Lucky Key Game
and get

HOW TO PLAY:

1. With a coin, carefully scratch off gold area at the right. Then check the claim chart to see what we have for you — **FREE BOOKS** and a **FREE GIFT** — **ALL YOURS FREE!**

2. Send back this card and you'll receive brand-new Silhouette Romance® novels. These books have a cover price of $3.50 each in the U.S. and $3.99 each in Canada, but they are yours to keep absolutely free.

3. There's no catch. You're under no obligation to buy anything. We charge nothing — ZERO — for your first shipment. And you don't have to make any minimum number of purchases — not even one!

4. The fact is thousands of readers enjoy receiving books by mail from the Silhouette Reader Service™ months before they're available in stores. They like the convenience of home delivery and they love our discount prices!

5. We hope that after receiving your free books you'll want to remain a subscriber. But the choice is yours — to continue or cancel, any time at all! So why not take us up on our invitation, with no risk of any kind. You'll be glad you did!

YOURS FREE!
A SURPRISE MYSTERY GIFT

We can't tell you what it is...but we're sure you'll like it! A
FREE GIFT—
just for playing the LUCKY KEY game!

FREE GIFTS!

NO COST! NO OBLIGATION TO BUY!
NO PURCHASE NECESSARY!

The Silhouette Reader Service™ — Here's how it works:

Accepting your 2 free books and gift places you under no obligation to buy anything. You may keep the books and gift and return the shipping statement marked "cancel." If you do not cancel, about a month later we'll send you 6 additional novels and bill you just $2.90 each in the U.S., or $3.25 each in Canada, plus 25¢ delivery per book and applicable taxes if any.* That's the complete price and — compared to cover prices of $3.50 each in the U.S. and $3.99 each in Canada — it's quite a bargain! You may cancel at any time, but if you choose to continue, every month we'll send you 6 more books, which you may either purchase at the discount price or return to us and cancel your subscription.

*Terms and prices subject to change without notice. Sales tax applicable in N.Y. Canadian residents will be charged applicable provincial taxes and GST.

If offer card is missing write to: Silhouette Reader Service, 3010 Walden Ave., P.O. Box 1867, Buffalo, NY 14240-1867

BUSINESS REPLY MAIL
FIRST-CLASS MAIL   PERMIT NO. 717   BUFFALO, NY

POSTAGE WILL BE PAID BY ADDRESSEE

SILHOUETTE READER SERVICE
3010 WALDEN AVE
PO BOX 1867
BUFFALO NY 14240-9952

NO POSTAGE
NECESSARY
IF MAILED
IN THE
UNITED STATES

brightly and only served to remind Gabe of just how impossible a marriage between them truly was.

She was a princess. He was her bodyguard. He'd gone above and beyond the limit to do just that...guard her body. But he couldn't bind himself to her forever. Despite the obvious opposition to such an event, his heart rebelled at the thought of being hurt another time.

Besides, he reminded himself firmly, it wasn't as if he loved Serena.

No matter that they were, for the moment, married. No matter that kissing her had stirred crazy emotions he'd thought were dead. He refused—absolutely refused—to fall in love with Princess Serena Wyndham.

From the moment they had gotten into the car and Gabe had told her they were going to the chapel to be married, Serena had felt as if she'd stepped into an alternate universe.

When he'd kissed her, she knew somehow she'd transcended from earth and fallen into paradise. The kiss had been more...so much more than she'd ever fantasized, ever hoped for. His lips had been so soft, yet masterful, sweeping her away with love and desire.

The wedding had been all that she'd ever wanted in a ceremony...except she wasn't sure exactly why the groom had married her. She wanted to believe it was because he loved her desperately, passionately. She wanted to believe that thoughts of her and

Avery had driven Gabe over the edge and he'd suddenly realized how much he loved her.

But since the ceremony ended, he hadn't acted like a newly wedded groom who was madly in love with his bride. He'd been distant and seemed far too eager to join the New Year's Eve melee than spend private time with his wife.

She sipped her champagne and noticed how the lights caught and sparkled on her ring. Her wedding band. She was married…married to Gabe. Her heart trilled a song of joy. She was Gabe's wife. Serena Morgan. It sounded perfect, as though the two names belonged together.

As the band began to play a slow song, she looked at Gabe…her husband, and she wanted him to dance with her. She wanted to be held tight in his big, safe arms as their bodies swayed to the rhythm of the music.

"Dance with me, Gabe," she said. He frowned, and she had a feeling he was about to lodge a protest. She didn't allow it. She stood and grabbed his hand. "Please. Every bride should get the pleasure of dancing with her groom."

He hesitated only a moment, then with a nod, he stood and took her arm to lead her to the dance floor. The music was slow and romantic, and the ring on Serena's finger, coupled with the glass of champagne she'd drunk far too quickly, made her more bold than she normally would be.

She wound her arms around his neck and pressed herself against him. For a brief moment he held himself rigid, as if in an attempt to keep distance between their bodies. With a nearly inaudible groan, he relaxed and wrapped his arms around her waist, accepting her body molding to his own.

She lay her head against his chest and closed her eyes. For so long she'd dreamed of being in Gabe's arms and now her dream was a reality. She had other dreams…fantasies of making love to him, bearing his children, growing old with him. Was tonight the prelude to all her dreams coming true? Her heart thudded in anticipation at the very thought.

Her heart wasn't the only one beating rapidly. She could feel Gabe's heart pounding a frenzied cadence. Was it possible he wanted her as much as she wanted him? The thought thrilled her.

All too soon the song ended and the band picked up the tempo with a fast hit from the fifties. Together, Serena and Gabe made their way back toward their table. They had almost reached their seats when Avery Kintell appeared.

"Sarah…darling…I've been looking for you everywhere," Avery exclaimed. Worry lines etched deep in his forehead as he took Serena's right hand in his. "Where have you been?"

Serena emitted a little forced laugh. "Avery, you aren't going to believe what happened," she said. "Gabe and I got married."

Avery stared at her for a moment, then threw back his head and laughed. "Oh, darling, you're such a funny girl. Why don't you come over here where I have a table waiting for us?"

"She's not going anywhere with you, Kintell. It's

true. We're married,'' Gabe said as he stepped next to Serena and took her arm in his.

Serena watched the two men glare at each other. They looked as if they were passing secret messages with their eyes.

"Avery, I'm terribly sorry," Serena said in an attempt to break the tension. "Gabe…it was all so sudden…so overwhelming."

"I'm sure it was," Avery said thinly. His eyes, when they gazed at her, were no longer friendly, but rather filled with animosity. "See you around," he finally said.

"I doubt it," Gabe returned evenly.

Serena and Gabe both watched Avery lose himself in the crowd, then Gabe smiled down at her. "Come on, let's go back to the table and share a toast."

The coldness that Avery's gaze had created in her dissipated beneath the warmth of Gabe's smile. They went back to their table where Gabe poured them each a glass of the bubbly champagne.

"To the future," he said and clinked his glass with hers.

Serena tamped down her disappointment. He hadn't said to "our" future, but rather to "the" future. Again, she wondered what had prompted the marriage. Suddenly she didn't want to go back to their room, where Gabe had said he would explain everything.

She wanted to stay right here and pretend that he'd married her because he loved her. She wanted to dance the night away in his arms, allow her fantasy of a future together to last for as long as possible.

When they finished the toast, Gabe signaled the waiter and ordered himself a glass of soda at the same time he poured Serena another serving of champagne.

"You don't drink," Serena said when the waiter had departed. "Other than the champagne you just had, I've never seen you have an alcoholic beverage. Why?"

"For several reasons," he replied. "The main reason is because I've always been on duty when I've been with you. The second reason is because there was a time in my life when I drank too much."

"You were an alcoholic?" Serena asked in surprise.

"Let's just say it was easy and appealing to lose myself in a bottle of scotch."

"Why would you want to do that?" Serena realized that although Gabe had been her bodyguard and despite the fact that at this moment they were man and wife, she knew very little about him and his past.

"For reasons far too complicated to go into at a New Year's Eve party," he replied, his eyes dark, forbidding her to push the issue.

Frustration nagged at her. How could she expect to develop any kind of intimacy with Gabe if he refused to share the pieces of his past that made him the man he was today?

What really frustrated her was that she had a feeling that was exactly why Gabe withheld pieces of himself, so that no intimacy could develop between them.

She twisted her wedding band around her finger. So why had he married her? Let him love me, she prayed with a hint of desperation. Let him love me just a little bit.

As midnight approached, Gabe placed the cardboard top hat on his head and together he and Serena joined the other partiers counting down the clock to midnight.

When the clock hands hit the hour, heralding in a new year, the band struck up *Auld Lang Syne* and Serena moved into Gabe's arms. She didn't give him a chance to protest, refused to consider that he wouldn't want to kiss her.

She raised up on her tiptoes, wound her arms around his neck and pulled his head down so her lips could meet his.

She felt his hesitation, but it lasted only a moment, then his arms wrapped around her, pulling her against his hard length as his mouth moved against hers.

Hot flames danced inside her, shooting up her arms, down her legs, exploding in the pit of her stomach like fireballs of desire.

She was vaguely aware of the hoots and hollers of the people around them, but they seemed distant and unreal as she reveled in Gabe's kiss. His tongue moved into her mouth, dancing erotically with hers, as he deepened the kiss.

All the sensations that had been missing when she'd kissed Avery were present with Gabe. Bells and whistles and smoke and fire—she was drowning in sensation and didn't want to come up for air.

All too quickly she did surface. Gabe ended the kiss and stepped back from her. For a moment his eyes appeared glazed and unfocused. He gave a tiny shake of his head and frowned. "We need to go upstairs," he said, his voice slightly unsteady. "We definitely need to talk."

They left the party and rode the elevator up to their room. Neither spoke, and Serena found the silence deafening. What did he think they needed to talk about? Whatever he felt he had to say, she instinctively knew she didn't want to hear it.

When they got into the suite, Serena headed right for her bedroom. "I'll be right back," she said to him. "Then we can talk about whatever you want."

Her hands shook as she closed the door to her room and contemplated what she intended to do. This was her wedding night and she wanted it to be as perfect, as special as any night she would ever experience in her life.

With this in mind, she undressed and slipped into the most luxurious, sexiest nightgown she owned. The mint-green gown slid down her body, caressing her curves in cool silk.

She reached up and unpinned her hair, then shook her head, allowing her curls to fall in a spill down her shoulders. She sprayed a spritz of her favorite perfume around her head, then checked her reflection in the mirror.

She was self-consciously aware that the deep, plunging neckline of the nightgown did little to hide her breasts, and the material was thin enough that each and every curve was visible.

Never before had Gabe seen her in anything so revealing, so sexy. But never before had they been married, she reminded herself. And the ring on her finger gave her courage…the courage to turn away from the mirror and leave the privacy of her room.

"What have you done?" Gabe said the moment he saw her, his voice once again thick and unsteady.

"What do you mean?" she replied, then gave a nonchalant shrug. "I just got ready for bed."

While she'd been in her bedroom, he'd taken off his jacket and tie and had loosened the collar of his shirt. He now tugged at the top of the shirt, as if still finding it too tight. "Do you always sleep in something like that?" he asked crossly.

"You don't like it?" She twirled around slowly to give him full view of the clingy, sensual gown. "I wanted to look nice for you, Gabe. I wanted to look beautiful for our wedding night."

He frowned and raked a hand through his hair. "Serena…about this marriage," he began.

She gave him no opportunity to continue. Walking to him, she slipped her arms around his waist and placed her head against his broad chest. "Oh, Gabe, this marriage makes me happier than I've ever been in my life," she said softly.

She could hear his heart beating a rapid rhythm. She felt his muscles grow taut, the stir of desire that filled him. With a deep groan, he pulled her away from him and held her at arm's length.

"Serena, the marriage isn't real." His eyes were

the deepest brown she'd ever seen as he gazed at her intently.

"Of course it's real," she protested. "You placed a ring on my finger and said vows before a minister and God. We have a license that states we are man and wife."

"That's true." He released his hold on her shoulders and took several steps back from her. "But I married you to keep you safe. Serena, I care about you and wanted to make sure you didn't make any crazy mistakes. As long as we don't consummate the marriage, your father can annul it when we get back to Wynborough."

"But I don't want an annulment," she said, fighting against tears that suddenly pressed hot and burdensome behind her eyelids.

"Serena, I care enough about you to make sure an annulment occurs." He averted his gaze from hers, as if he found it difficult to talk to her while looking at her. "I'm not husband material, Serena. I told you before I don't have a heart. You deserve somebody better in your life. Now, I'm going to bed. I'll see you in the morning."

Without waiting for her reply, he turned and went into his bedroom, closing the door behind him. Serena stood and stared at the closed door, the first of her tears trekking down her cheeks.

She loved him. The moment he had slipped the gold band on her finger, she'd recognized and embraced the love in her heart for him.

Angrily, she swiped at her tears and moved to stand at the windows. The night lights of Las Vegas glittered and shone, but the brightness only served to make her feel lonely.

It was her wedding night. It should be the happiest night of her life, but instead she'd never felt more lonely. Her husband was in his room, and he expected her to sleep in her own room...alone...apart from him.

He'd said he cared about her, a little voice reminded her. He'd said he cared, and the two kisses they'd shared spoke of an emotion deeper, more complex. He wanted her. She'd felt it when he held her while they'd danced; she'd known it when she'd entered the room in her nightgown and his eyes had glowed with a feverish light.

If they made love, there was no way an annulment could occur. If he cared about her, wanted her, then surely she could make him love her.

The tears halted as her thoughts raced. She wanted Gabriel Morgan, not just for a night, not just for a week, but for a lifetime. She was spirited and willful, and she almost always got what she wanted. Gabriel Morgan didn't stand a chance.

She went into her bedroom and grabbed her pillow from her bed, then padded back to Gabe's bedroom door. She could make this marriage real. She could make it work.

All she had to do was seduce her husband.

Chapter Seven

Gabe slid beneath the sheets of his bed, knowing
sleep would be difficult. It would be impossible to
surrender to slumber with the vision of Serena in
that sexy nightgown still emblazoned on his brain.

The pale green gown had intensified the emerald
of her eyes and had barely skimmed her breasts,
revealing more than it concealed. It was a gown created to make a man want to take it off, a gown
formulated to stir mind-boggling passion. It had
worked.

Not only did he have her stunning image in his
head, but the taste of her still lingered on his mouth;
the warmth of her body pressed against his own still
teased him with possibilities.

The marriage had been a mistake. He knew that
now. But at the time it had seemed the only logical
solution to the problem of Avery Kintell's machi-

nations and Serena's own impetuousness. But, as usual, he'd not counted on Serena's response to the whole thing.

She was the most complicated, bewildering woman he'd ever met. She never reacted the way he expected, usually surprising him and reminding him of her complexity.

One thing was certain. He had to stay true to his original plan. He and Serena were married, but he intended it to remain a marriage in name only. As long as they didn't make love, King Phillip could annul the marriage as soon as they returned home.

Then Serena would be free to find a man whose heart was open and giving, a man who would love her to distraction. And Gabe…he'd continue alone, as he'd been for the last four years…alone and safe from any hurt life might throw his way.

He jumped upright as his bedroom door opened. He smelled her, although the room was too dark for him to see her. She smelled of the exotic, spicy perfume that always caused his head to spin.

"Serena, what are you doing?" he asked, tensed for any possibility.

"I know you don't intend to consummate our marriage, but that doesn't mean I can't sleep with my husband." The opposite side of the bed depressed with her weight.

Gabe wanted to protest. He wanted to rocket out of the bed to escape the scent of her, the knowledge that she was right next to him in that gown that would be cool and slick beneath his hands, and the skin beneath that would be invitingly warm.

"Relax, Gabe," she said as if reading his thoughts. "I promise I won't force you to make love to me." Her voice softened somewhat. "I just don't want to sleep alone, okay. A woman shouldn't have to sleep alone on her wedding night."

How he wanted to toss her out, lock the door behind her so she couldn't get to him. He heard the rustle of the sheets as she got comfortable. Every nerve he possessed was on guard, wary of her and more wary of his own control where she was concerned.

"Are you tired?" she asked, her voice a soft whisper in the darkness of the room.

"Exhausted," he replied.

"So I guess you don't want to talk."

The last thing he wanted to do was hear her voice. If he heard her, then he couldn't ignore that she was lying right next to him. "No, I don't want to talk," he replied.

In fact, he wished he didn't have to breathe, so he couldn't smell her. He wished he couldn't feel, so her body warmth didn't invade his space.

"Good night, Gabe," she said, her voice soft and sweet, as if she had no idea of the raging emotions her very nearness stirred in him.

"Good night," he replied and lowered himself back to the mattress. He was careful not to twitch a muscle, move a leg or an arm onto her side. He had a feeling if he touched her in any fashion, no matter how innocuous, it would snap the tenuous hold he had on his self-control.

She sighed, a soft sound that somehow spoke of

wistfulness, of yearning. Gabe squeezed his eyes tightly closed and prayed for sleep.

Within thirty minutes, Serena was fast asleep. Gabe remained tense, listening to her deep, rhythmic breathing. What was she doing in here with him? What had prompted her to come to his bed, knowing that he'd made it clear he didn't want to make love to her?

Sleep didn't come to Gabe until near dawn, and he awoke with the sun seeping around the edges of the drawn curtains. At some point, in the brief time they'd both been asleep, their bodies had sought each other.

Gabe lay on his back, Serena's head on his chest, her one arm across his chest. Her body was curled up next to his, one leg thrown across his thighs. It was obvious that at some point her nightgown had worked its way up her body, for the leg that was across him was bare.

He knew he should get up, get away from the sweet warmth of her, but she was still sleeping, and for just a moment he wanted the pleasure of her in his arms.

Her hair smelled like flowers, with a hint of sweet shampoo, and her body radiated a sleepy warmth that was bewitching.

He closed his eyes once again, fighting the overwhelming desire to awaken her with a kiss, to pull her to consciousness by stroking down the length of her. He could imagine the surprise and pleasure that would light her sleep-filled eyes as he caressed her breasts, then kissed each and every inch of her.

Desire surged inside him, a desire so intense it nearly stole his breath away. Heaven help him, but he wanted her. He ran a hand up her arm, her skin achingly soft. It was more than lust that stirred in him. Lust would have him take her without regard for her mental well-being. Lust would have him sate his need without thinking of the heartache he might inflict on her.

But reservations kept his lust in check, and the fact that he had any reservations about making love to her let him know his feelings for her were much more complex than mere want.

He needed to contact Lieutenant Breckenridge today to find out if the man had been successful in locating Betty Jo Parker. The quicker they found the woman, the faster they'd get back to Wynborough and the faster he would be released from the marriage he'd foolishly entered.

Serena stirred against him and he tensed, knowing she was leaving behind her dreams and surfacing to the new day. She raised her head and smiled, a sweet, open smile that soared through him. "Good morning," she said, but didn't move away from him. "Did you sleep well?"

"Not really," he replied gruffly. "You've been crowding me all night long."

"Oh, sorry." Languidly she moved away from him and stretched like a contented cat. Her motion caused the sheet to fall away, exposing to his gaze one perfect silk-clad breast.

He started to get out of bed, desire roaring in his

head, but she grabbed his arm. "Don't go," she said.

"I'm awake. I always get out of bed when I'm awake," he countered. Relief filled him as she pulled the sheet up around her neck.

"Please, stay here and talk to me for a little while." Her eyes held a soft appeal, and with the sheets completely covering her she was less threatening to him. "You were too tired to talk last night, but you can't be tired now."

"Talk about what?" he asked, still unsure it was wise to linger in the bed with her.

"Stuff. Anything and everything." She rolled over on her side to face him and propped a pillow beneath her head. She frowned, still managing to look sexy with her hair disheveled and her cheeks slightly flushed. "If you won't make love to me, the least you can do is talk to me. That's what married people do."

She had no clue what marriage truly entailed…the giving of hearts without reservation, the mingling of souls so that you no longer knew where you left off and your mate began. But if talking would make her happy, he'd talk.

He settled back and eyed her expectantly. "Okay, let's talk."

She smiled, flashing that quicksilver dimple at the corner of her mouth. "About what?"

He laughed despite his discomfort and shook his head. "It's your game, Princess."

"Tell me about you…you mentioned before that

you don't have any family. What happened to your parents?''

"They died in a car wreck when I was two."

"Oh, Gabe. I'm so sorry." Her face radiated sorrow for him.

"Don't be," he said, touched by her empathy. "I don't remember them, and it's difficult to miss something you never really had."

"Then who raised you?" she asked curiously.

"I was raised in foster homes."

"Gabe...that's so sad," she said.

He smiled at her. Despite her stubbornness and willfulness, he knew she had a soft heart. "It wasn't so sad," he replied. "I stayed in some good places, and I stayed in some not so good places, but I survived."

"Childhood should be about more than survival," she exclaimed.

"My childhood made me strong," he returned. "It made me realize I couldn't depend on anyone but myself."

"That kind of strength carried too far becomes a weakness," she said softly.

He eyed her sharply, surprised by her perception. "Maybe," he agreed. "But it's a safe weakness."

"It's a sad weakness," she countered.

The conversation had spun out of his control, and was now touching areas he didn't want touched. He wasn't weak; he was smart and she'd never understand that because she'd never known tragedy, never known the ache of loss.

He'd learned in his early years that the people in

his life weren't permanent. Just when he'd start to feel safe, to let down his guard and care about the parents he'd been placed with, he'd be moved to a new family. By the time he was ten, he had already erected a barrier around his heart...a barrier that had been breached by only one woman, and in the end, she'd abandoned him, too.

He rolled out of bed, not liking the direction of his thoughts. Serena's questions had him thinking too much. "I'm going to take a shower," he said.

"Okay. I'll order some breakfast," Serena said.

He was grateful she didn't try to stop him as he went into the bathroom. He locked the door behind him, not trusting her. Knowing Serena, she'd decide she wanted to bathe with him. He could just hear her saying that she knew they weren't going to make love, but at least they could shower together. It was what married people did together.

Despite his earlier unhappy thoughts, he smiled and shook his head ruefully as he thought of Serena. She seemed to have very definite ideas of what being married entailed.

Although Gabe was thirty years old, only nine years older than Serena, there were times he felt a hundred years older than her in life experience.

As he stood beneath the warm spray of water, he thought of all the events that had led him to work for King Phillip. After LeAnn's death, Gabe had plunged into a despair so black, he'd thought he would never surface from it. A picture in a travel agency window of Wynborough's rugged cliffs and charming villages had prompted his impulsive trip to the small country.

During the days, he'd worked security at one of the casinos, and during the long, lonely nights, he'd drank himself into a stupor. Then he'd come to King Phillip's attention and had worked as head of security in the palace.

When the King had offered him the position as head of the Royal Wynborough Bodyguards, Gabe had a feeling he'd taken the job in an attempt to be redeemed. While he protected all the princesses, Gabe had made Serena his top priority, realizing that decision had been a further need for redemption. He had not been able to guard his wife and keep her safe, but in these past months of keeping Serena safe, Gabe had found a measure of forgiveness for himself.

Somehow, in the months of being with Serena, his deep, internal wounds had healed. He would always feel a natural sadness when he thought of LeAnn, but thoughts of her no longer ripped him apart.

However, just because his pain had dissipated didn't mean he was willing to make himself vulnerable again. He would never allow himself to love another person again. He would never be that kind of fool again.

He shut off the water and dried off, resolved that he could remain strong where Serena was concerned. He cared about her, he knew he desired her, but he would never really love her as she needed to be loved. He'd take her back to her father, have the marriage annulled, then she could get on with her life and find a man who would love her desperately, passionately, as she longed to be loved.

He left the bathroom, dressed for the day and found Serena already seated at the table, nibbling on a piece of toast from the breakfast cart. She was still clad in the bewitching nightgown, but thankfully, she'd pulled on a matching robe that covered her from neck to ankles.

"I poured you coffee," she said with a sunshine smile. "And I ordered you scrambled eggs. The morning paper is on the cart, too."

"Thanks." He fixed himself a plate, then grabbed the paper and sat down across from her.

She smiled and again he was struck by her beauty. With the golden light of the morning sun playing on her hair and her cheeks filled with color, she looked sexy and touchable and far too appealing.

"This is our first breakfast together as husband and wife," she said.

"Serena—"

"I know. According to you, it isn't a real marriage," she interrupted. "But that doesn't change the fact that for the moment we are married and this is our first breakfast together since our wedding."

"Okay…you're right," he agreed helplessly.

He took a sip of his coffee and opened the morning paper. He stared at the headline and the accompanying picture. "Oh my God," he exclaimed, a sinking feeling in the pit of his stomach.

"What's wrong?" Serena asked.

Wordlessly, Gabe shoved the paper over in front

of her. Serena stared at the front page. Did They Or Didn't They? the headline screamed. The picture was of the two of them in front of Ye Olde Wedding Chapel and it had obviously been taken as they had exited after the ceremony, for their gold bands on their fingers were easily visible.

"Who...how?" Serena sputtered with surprise.

"Apparently we were followed by a photographer or reporter who knew who we were and smelled a story." Gabe let loose an expletive and shoved away from the table to stand.

"At least it's a good picture of us," Serena said. Secretly, she was rather pleased. Other people knowing they were married made it all seem much more real.

"A good picture?" Gabe glared at her.

She flushed. "Don't be mad at me," she exclaimed. "I didn't take the photo and sell it to the paper." Serena scanned the article. "It's all speculation. Edward Doyle refused to admit or deny that we were there to get married."

"It doesn't matter whether it's speculation or not. We have to call your parents right away. It wouldn't be fair for them to hear it through the grapevine and not from us." Gabe's frown let Serena know he dreaded telling her parents.

"We would have had to tell them at some point," she reminded him.

"I know," he agreed, more calm than before. "I just don't like feeling manipulated by a reporter. I would have preferred to pick the time and place to tell your parents. But it appears the time has been chosen for me, and the time is right now.''

He strode across the room and picked up the phone. Serena knew he had the number to her father's private line, and she assumed that was what he punched in. The connection took a moment.

''Sir, it's Gabriel,'' Gabe said when the connection finally clicked through.

As Gabe spoke with her father, Serena sipped her coffee and watched him. Waking up in his arms that morning had been the most wonderful thing she'd ever experienced.

She had feigned sleep for several minutes after awakening, allowing the sensations of his nearness to sweep over her, through her. His body had been toasty warm, and the feel of his bare skin against hers had made her want to weep with want.

When he'd run his hand softly up her arm in a caress that held infinite softness, a wealth of tenderness, her love for him had filled her. She'd hoped that he would continue touching her, let his touching grow more intimate, allow the passion she knew he felt for her to spin out of control. But he hadn't.

Now, standing near the window, with the sun playing on his features, he looked strong and determined and she loved him for his strength, and hated him for it as well. If he wasn't so strong, perhaps his desire for her would careen out of control. If he wasn't so strong, maybe he'd find some little piece of love for her in his heart.

''Yes, sir,'' Gabe said into the receiver. ''I have everything under control, but we wanted you to hear about it from us rather than from a news article. There were some complications and immediate action was necessary.''

Complications. Immediate action was necessary. The words arrowed through Serena's heart. Had Gabe's vows only been uttered in the line of duty? Without any emotion at all? Would he ever love her as she loved him?

Gabe looked at Serena and a slight flush colored his cheeks. ''She will be returned to you safely and the marriage will not be consummated so an annulment can be obtained immediately upon our return to Wynborough.''

Gabe averted his gaze from her and instead focused out the window as the conversation continued. ''No problem. Okay…here she is.'' He held out the receiver to Serena. ''Your mother wants to talk to you.''

Serena walked over and took the phone. ''Mama?''

''Darling, are you all right?'' Queen Gabriella's voice washed over Serena with love and concern. Serena closed her eyes, surprised to feel the heat of tears.

No, I'm not all right, she wanted to confess. I have made the stupidest mistake by falling helplessly in love with Gabe and my heart is going to be broken by him. She said none of it, knowing that there were some things a mother, even a mother who was a queen, couldn't fix.

''I'm fine,'' she assured her mom.

''Your father wanted to talk to you, but he had to

leave for a meeting. Serena, darling, have you been giving Gabriel a difficult time?''

"No more than usual," Serena replied and Queen Gabriella laughed.

Suddenly Serena wished she were home, where her mother could wrap her in a loving embrace. And yet she didn't want to go home, because going home meant losing Gabe.

"When are you coming home, Serena?" Queen Gabriella asked.

"Soon," Serena replied. "Probably in the next week or two." She forced a lightness to her tone. "You know we're all busy promoting Wynborough and the upcoming celebration of father's coronation." The last thing she wanted her parents to know was that the four princesses were hunting down leads to their brother's whereabouts.

After another few minutes of talking, Serena said her goodbyes and hung up the phone. She returned to the table and gestured for Gabe to do the same. "So, what was my father's reaction?" she asked when he'd joined her.

He shrugged. "Surprisingly well. Of course, I was quick to explain to him all the reasons for the marriage and the fact that it isn't a 'real' marriage. I'm sure he wouldn't be thrilled to have a royal bodyguard as his actual son-in-law."

Serena looked at him in surprise. "I can promise you that my father's first concern would be for my happiness," she exclaimed. "He wouldn't care whether I married a royal bodyguard or a shoe salesman, if that's what made me happy."

Gabe looked at her in disbelief. "Surely you don't really believe that," he scoffed.

A little niggling doubt entered her mind, but she shoved it aside. "I not only believe it, I know for certain that it's true." Serena leaned forward. "My father is a man who places great value on love, not on position or a person's station in life."

Serena's heart filled with love as she thought of her father, the most loving, just, wise man she'd ever known. However, she couldn't forget that her father was also king and never forgot what was best for his people, his country. But, she needed to believe that her father's first concern would be her happiness. She needed to believe that it wouldn't matter if she married her bodyguard.

"If my father didn't believe in true love, he never would have married a salesclerk."

Gabe's eyes widened in surprise. "When did your father marry a salesclerk?" he asked.

"When he married my mother," Serena answered with a sense of satisfaction.

Gabe's face radiated amazement. "Queen Gabriella was a salesclerk?"

Serena nodded. "In Aspen. She sold glassware and jewelry in the resort areas around Aspen." Serena smiled as she remembered how often she'd asked her mother to relate the story to her. "The first time my father saw her, he was completely smitten with her. He had to have her and he refused to take no for an answer." She shivered, wishing Gabe felt that way about her.

"I never knew that," he replied.

"The whole point of the story is that my father believes in the power and glory of love and I know as long as I'm happy and in love, he won't care who the man is or what he does for a living."

"Good. Then when you find that special shoe salesman, or whoever, you know you'll have your father's blessing." He stood, ignoring her look of frustration. He went over to the window and stared out, his rigid back making him appear stiff and unyielding.

Serena sighed. What he didn't understand was that she didn't want a shoe salesman. She didn't want a prince or a duke. All she wanted was Gabriel Morgan.

She wondered if the little pieces of his past that he'd shared with her that morning had anything to do with his continuous assertions that he didn't have a heart. Had growing up in foster care made him afraid to trust others? Afraid to love?

She'd meant what she'd told him. Being strong was a valuable asset, but taken to the extreme, it became a liability.

Was he afraid to allow his feelings freedom? Afraid to love her?

What a pair they made. He was afraid to love her and she was afraid he wouldn't love her.

She got up from the table and approached him. He didn't turn around, but remained staring out the window with his back to her.

She walked up behind him, put her arms around his waist and laid her head against his back. He tensed.

"Serena…what are you doing?"

"Just giving you a hug," she replied. "I think maybe when you were growing up, you didn't get all the hugs you needed."

He stood motionless, neither rejecting, nor accepting her hug. His stillness was so complete, for a moment she thought he'd stopped breathing.

Serena wanted to soothe all the hurt he'd ever experienced as a child. She understood the kind of empty loneliness he must have felt and she wanted to heal him.

Still not saying a word, Gabe gently disentangled her arms from his waist, then turned to face her. His features were softened and he reached out and drew a thumb down her cheek. "For a spoiled brat, you can be incredibly giving." His voice was deep, a soft caress as potent as his touch on her face.

Serena sensed his defenses were down, that at least for this moment his heart was open and available to her. She reached up and touched his cheek, as he had touched hers. She wanted to tell him how deep her love for him was, how complete loving him made her feel. She wanted to tell him not to be afraid, that she would love him until the end of time, but she was afraid she'd chase him away.

His eyes were dark and he lowered his head toward hers. She knew he was going to kiss her and she desperately wanted him to.

He'd kissed her at the end of their wedding ceremony and again at midnight on New Year's Eve, but this would be the first kiss initiated by him, initiated by his desire and not any other circumstances.

She raised up on her tiptoes to accept his kiss, then the phone rang.

He jumped away from her as if shocked by a cattle prod. Serena swallowed a scream of frustration. As he answered the phone, she stared out the window, bitterly disappointed.

It had been a single, shining moment. His heart had been unlocked, accessible to her. She'd seen it in his eyes, felt it in his touch. And now the moment had been lost.

She turned to face him as he hung up the phone.

"That was Lieutenant Breckenridge," Gabe said. "He found Betty Jo Parker for us."

Chapter Eight

It was almost two hours later when Gabe and Serena entered the Treasure Chest Casino in downtown Las Vegas. As they walked toward the office, Gabe could feel the nervous energy radiating from Serena.

The phone call from Lieutenant Breckenridge couldn't have come at a more opportune time. Gabe didn't want to think about what might have happened had the phone not rung. But he knew with certainty he'd been about to make a huge mistake.

Her hug had touched him deeply, more so than anything else in his life that he could remember. It had been such a simple gesture, yet he knew it had been a spontaneous gift from her heart.

As they reached the casino office, Serena placed a hand on his arm. "Give me just a minute," she said, and leaned against the wall to draw in deep breaths. She gave him a small, trembling smile. "All of a sudden, I'm so nervous. It's possible in the next few minutes we'll know where James is.'' Her smile fell away. ''It's New Year's Day. Maybe Betty isn't working.''

''Breckenridge said she's here.'' Gabe shoved his hands in his pockets, fighting the desire to kiss the nervous tremble from her lips, kiss her until her mouth trembled with another emotion. ''This is why you came to Las Vegas. This is what you've been waiting for.''

''I know...and that's why I'm so nervous.'' She reached over and tugged his hand out of his pocket and grasped it tightly. ''Oh, Gabe, I want this so badly. I want to give my parents back their son. I want James back in our lives.''

Gabe placed an arm around her shoulder, wanting to support her. She could be the most irritating woman he'd ever known, but she also had the softest heart of anyone he'd ever met.

He knew her need to find James wasn't just her own, but rather a desire for her to give her parents back the son they had lost so many years before.

''I just hope she knows where James is,'' Serena said.

''She won't know James by his real name,'' Gabe reminded her.

Serena nodded. ''I hope she knows where Bill Lewis is, and I hope Bill Lewis is James.''

Gabe gave her a quick hug, then released his hold on her. ''You ready?'' he asked.

She drew one more deep breath, then nodded and together they went into the office. They spoke to a supervisor, who eyed them suspiciously, then asked if Betty was in trouble.

"No trouble at all," Serena quickly responded. "It's a family matter," she explained. "We just need to talk to her for a minute or two."

The supervisor, a big man with a bald head, eyed her for a long moment, then nodded, as if satisfied there would be no trouble. "Betty is in the lounge. She's the bartender."

"Thank you," Serena said and was halfway out the office door before Gabe could catch up to her.

The lounge was connected to the casino through an inner door. Gabe and Serena followed the signs and entered the small, adjoining room. Despite the morning hour, there were already people in the lounge. Several men sat on the stools at the bar, and two couples sat at two of the tables that dotted the room.

A woman stood behind the bar, wiping out a glass as she talked to one of the men seated there. She was short, rather plump and wrinkles radiated from her sharp eyes. Her hair was short, with gray strands intermingling with a darker brown.

Before Gabe could approach the woman, Serena grabbed his arm and tugged him to sit down with her at a table. "Something's wrong," she said.

He looked at her curiously. "What are you talking about?"

She shot a meaningful glance to the bartender, then looked back at Gabe. "If that's Betty Jo Parker, then something is definitely wrong."

"I don't understand. What's the matter?" Gabe asked.

She looked at the bartender again, a worried frown marring the smooth skin of her forehead. She nibbled her lower lip worriedly, then said, "Katherine thought that Betty Jo Parker was Bill Lewis's lover, but that woman looks too old."

"Too old for what?" Gabe smiled at her. "Too old to love? Too old to be romantically involved?"

"If Bill Lewis is James, then he's only thirty years old, and that woman looks like she's in her mid-fifties."

Gabe smiled patiently. "Perhaps your brother is like your father and believes in the power of love...a love that transcends age barriers."

"I guess you could be right," she said, once again catching her lower lip between her teeth.

"The only way you're going to find out is to go over and talk to the woman," Gabe said gently. He knew she was afraid...afraid that once again the possibility of finding James would be lost.

Serena drew one last deep breath, nodded and stood. Gabe followed just behind her as she made her way to two stools at the bar. As she slid onto one, Gabe sat on the other.

"Morning, folks," Betty said as she moved down to stand before them. "What can I get you?" she asked with a friendly smile.

"A little information," Gabe said.

Betty's graying eyebrows rose slightly and the smile wavered. "Information about what?"

"Bill Lewis," Serena replied. "Do you know him?"

"Is Bill in trouble?" Betty asked, worry creating lines across her forehead.

"Not that we're aware of," Gabe answered truthfully.

Betty swiped the top of the bar once again. "Then why do you want to know where he is?"

Serena drew a deep breath before answering. "We're looking for Bill because we believe he might be my long-lost brother."

Betty shook her head. "That's impossible," she exclaimed.

"Why is it impossible? We know Bill was at The Sunshine Home for Children in Hope, Arizona, when my brother would have been. Bill is the right age. Everything points to him." There was a desperation in Serena's voice.

"Bill is an only child. He doesn't have any brothers or sisters. I should know. I'm Bill's mother."

"His mother," Serena gasped. She reached out blindly for Gabe's hand. He gripped hers tightly, knowing the bitter disappointment she must be feeling at that moment.

"Bill contacted me a couple of months ago," Betty explained softly, as if aware that Serena had been shattered by her news. "He found me through a private investigator. We talked to each other several times on the phone. Bill even gave me his partner's number in case I needed to find him. We had a lot of healing to do. He came out here to see me a while back. We had a nice visit, but recently I haven't heard or seen from him.''

With every word Betty spoke, Serena appeared to grow smaller, more fragile. Gabe had known that finding James was important. However, he hadn't realized just how much hope Serena had placed in Betty Jo Parker and Bill Lewis. It was evident now that Bill Lewis wasn't the crown prince and all of Serena's spirit seemed crushed beneath the knowledge.

''We're sorry we bothered you,'' Serena said dully. She let go of Gabe's hand and slid off the stool.

''Honey, I'm sorry I couldn't help you,'' Betty said. ''I hope you find your brother. I know how difficult it is to live each day when there's a piece missing from your heart.''

Gabe nodded their thanks to the woman and together he and Serena left the lounge. Serena managed to hold herself together through the drive back to the hotel and the short trip up in the elevator. But Gabe sensed the breakdown to come.

She was taut as a rope threatening to fray, as tight as a wire about to snap. For the first time in years, Gabe didn't want to run from the explosion of emotion he sensed she was about to release. Rather he wanted to be here for her, to hold her, to somehow ease the pain of her disappointment. It surprised him, this need of his to be her strength.

''I need to call my sisters,'' she said the moment they entered the suite. ''They need to know that Bill Lewis isn't James.'' She sat on the edge of the sofa and stared at the phone, as if reluctant to make the calls.

He nodded, fighting the desire to take her into his arms. She looked achingly fragile, but he knew Serena well enough to know that when she needed him, she'd reach out for him. Instead of following through on his desire to hold her, he sat next to her on the sofa.

He watched as she slowly punched in a series of numbers, then waited for her call to be answered.

"Katherine, it's me. Happy New Year to you, too." Serena twisted the phone cord around her fingers as she spoke. "I wanted to let you know that I found Betty Jo Parker. She wasn't Bill Lewis's lover as we suspected. She's Bill's mother. Bill isn't James."

As Serena explained the situation to Katherine, Gabe watched her. He'd seen Serena in a dozen moods in the past. He'd seen her fiery with anger or smoldering with aggravation. He'd seen her green eyes darken with hurt and dance with joy. But though he'd spent almost every hour of every day with Serena, he'd never seen her look as sad as she did at this moment.

It was a sadness that filled his heart, touched him in a way he hadn't been touched in a very long time. If it had been in his capacity, he would rush out and beat every bush, turn over every stone, never rest until he could present her with her long-lost brother.

He shifted positions as she dialed the phone again. Two more sisters to contact, he thought, then she would fall apart.

"Alexandra, it's me," she said, before relating her discovery to first her eldest sister, then to Elizabeth.

She unwound the cord and sat up straighter, listening to whatever Elizabeth was saying. "Really? That's great. I'll keep my fingers crossed." She shot a quick glance at Gabe, then looked back at the phone. "We'll probably be returning home to Wynborough in the next day or two. There's something I need to take care of. Yes, I'll keep in touch. Love you, too."

She hung up the receiver, then looked at Gabe once again. "Elizabeth has another promising lead to follow. While going through the records at The Sunshine Home, she came up with a few more names of boys who could be James. She asked Grandma Beulah about them and they've narrowed it down to one man. A man named Sam Flynn."

"That's great, but who is Grandma Beulah?" Gabe asked, sorry he hadn't kept up with all this from the very beginning. Besides, he thought, talking might give Serena an opportunity to calm down.

"I told you already. Grandma Beulah is a woman who used to work at The Sunshine Home. She'd been retired for years, but she's the one who found a blanket with our family crest and contacted Laura Bishop about it. She's the reason we started this whole search."

She stood from the sofa, her body still vibrating with energy, an energy that appeared unhealthy when coupled with the paleness of her face.

"Are you all right?" Gabe asked softly.

"I'm fine," she replied, and promptly burst into tears.

She was appalled. She hadn't even been aware the tears were coming. She was surprised when Gabe rose and walked over to enfold her in his arms. She buried her face into the crisp, masculine scent of his shirt. Her tears came faster, uncontrollably hard, and as sobs shook her, Gabe soothed her, rubbing his hands down her back and whispering words of comfort.

"I'm sorry, sweetheart. I'm so sorry you were disappointed." His deep voice caressed her, but instead of easing the flow of her tears, it only served to make her cry harder.

"Elizabeth told you they have other leads. We'll find James," he said.

She knew that he thought she was disappointed because Bill Lewis wasn't her brother.

He had no idea that she wasn't sure if her tears were for the brother she hadn't found or if her heart was breaking because now there was no other reason for them to remain in Las Vegas. Now they would travel back to Wynborough, where her father would grant them an annulment.

Somehow it had all become confused in her mind. But she knew one thing for certain. She was going to lose Gabe, and she knew losing him would break her heart forever. Although she knew now he'd married her for all the wrong reasons, she'd hoped that with a little time he would realize he loved her as deeply as she loved him.

Now they were all out of time.

This thought made her cry harder and she clung to Gabe, wishing he would hold her forever, through eternity. His arms were strong enough to protect her throughout her lifetime. His shoulders were broad enough to share any of her burdens. His laughter was deep enough, infectious enough to pull laughter from her. If only his heart was big enough, opened enough to love her just a little bit.

"Serena, honey, you've got to stop crying. You're going to make yourself ill," he finally said, worry deepening his voice.

She raised her head to look at him. "Kiss me, Gabe. Please, just kiss me."

His eyes darkened and he hesitated only a moment, then his lips claimed hers in a fiery kiss that stole every thought from her mind. His mouth was fire, and Serena wanted to be consumed by his flame.

Tears forgotten, she opened her mouth to him, allowing his tongue to deepen the kiss, at the same time she unbuttoned his jacket and attempted to shove it off his shoulders.

He aided her in the attempt, shrugging out of it and allowing it to fall to the floor. Her hands then found the buttons of his shirt. She fumbled to unfasten them, wanting—needing—to touch the heat of his skin. When she reached the bottom of the material, she tugged the shirt from his slacks and tore the offending barrier from him.

She was out of control and somewhere in the back of her mind, she knew it, reveled in it. Her only thought was of Gabe and her need to feel him next to her.

She knew he was out of control as well. His breathing came in quick gasps as his fingers found the buttons of her blouse. His mouth was everywhere, along her jaw, across her cheeks, then once again on her mouth.

Taking a step back from him, she pulled her unbuttoned blouse off, leaving her in only a pale pink lacy bra. She didn't want him to take her here, in the middle of the floor, or on the uncomfortable sofa. She wanted him in the bed...in their bed, where they had spent their first night as husband and wife.

She backed away from him, toward the bedroom as she reached behind her and unclasped her bra. She felt a brief moment of hesitation, of shyness, but reminded herself he was her husband. It didn't matter what had prompted the wedding ceremony. They were married, and she wanted her husband to make love to her. There was nothing wrong with that...rather there was something intrinsically right with it.

He appeared dazed, his eyes darker than she'd ever seen them before. Desire was written all over his features...a desire too strong to ignore, too potent to avoid.

As her bra came unfastened, she held it against her, still hiding her breasts from his view. She allowed it to drop to the floor as she stepped out of his view and into the bedroom.

She stood for a moment alone, heart thudding

frantically as she wondered if he'd follow her or if he'd find the strength to halt this loving process.

Her breath caught in her chest as he appeared in the doorway, filling the space with his overwhelming presence, filling the entire room with his masculinity.

As he stood there, his gaze burning into hers, she unfastened her slacks and slid them down her hips. She had never felt more feminine, more desirable than at this moment. Kicking the slacks to the side, she stood before him in nothing but a pair of silky panties.

Trembling with need, she held her breath as she waited to see if he'd deny her or accept what she knew had been inevitable for some time.

"Gabriel," she said softly, pleadingly.

Slowly, as if still dazed, his hands went to the fastening of his slacks. He unclasped, then unzipped them, the sound explosive in the otherwise silent room.

"Serena." Her name eased out of him with the reverence of a prayer. His slacks fell to the ground, exposing his long, athletic legs and the undeniable evidence of his desire for her.

And then they were in each other's arms, tumbling to the bed while their bodies pressed together and their mouths found each other's in a kiss that swept away all reason.

His skin was hot, heated with flames of desire. Serena ran her hands across his chest, tangled her fingers in the wiry hair, caressed down his flat, muscled abdomen.

Her heart sang with pleasure as his lips left hers and instead nipped at her breasts, taking the turgid tips in his mouth and creating sizzling sensations inside her.

Serena knew the intensity of her response to him was not only because of the mastery of his touch. It was because her love for him filled her up, made her whole, made her vulnerable yet unafraid to respond without reservation to each and every caress.

"I love you, Gabriel. I love you so much," she said, unable to repress what burned in her heart.

He froze, not moving a muscle. In that moment she realized that speaking her heart had been a terrible mistake.

She released a small cry as he rolled off her and stood. "I'm sorry, Serena. I shouldn't have let things get so out of control. This isn't going to happen now...or ever."

He turned and disappeared into the bathroom. She heard the click of the door locking behind him. Locked out. Out of his heart.

Her body ached with need, with want...with love. Tears burned at her eyes, pressing so hot, so thick, she couldn't swallow fast enough to make them go away. She gave into them. This time there was no confusion. She knew exactly why she cried. She cried for Gabe...because he didn't love her.

Chapter Nine

Gabe stood beneath a cold shower for an interminably long time, attempting to scrub away the feel of Serena's sweet, heated flesh against his own, to scour off the floral scent that lingered despite the soap and water.

His desire had spun out of control so quickly, he'd had no defenses. She'd been like a white-hot flame inside him searing away good sense and all reason, leaving behind only the incredible need to possess her.

Thank goodness good sense had prevailed. Her sweetly uttered words of love had returned sanity and halted what would have been an irreversible error on his part.

He finished his shower, wondering how he would be able to face Serena again and not think of the heat of her body against his, the honeyed taste of her lips, the perfect size of her breasts.

He dressed and left the bathroom, relieved to discover that Serena was no longer in his bed. In fact, she was nowhere in the suite.

Damn. Had she run off again? Had he shoved her out of his bed and into harm's way? He raced across the living area to her bedroom, then into her bathroom, but both rooms were empty. No sign of Serena anywhere.

He cursed her, then cursed himself. He hadn't a clue where to begin to look for her. Before he could fully work himself up, she walked through the door carrying a pizza box and a handful of tabloid papers.

"I thought we agreed you wouldn't leave here alone," he said as she set the pizza on the table.

"I was hoping to be back before you knew I'd left. I just went down the street. I was hungry for pizza."

She didn't look at him and he didn't have the heart to yell at her. Her eyes were red rimmed and slightly swollen, and it hurt him to know that he'd been the cause of her tears.

"You want some pizza?" She finally looked at him and he could see that she was struggling to keep things as normal as possible between them.

"Sure," he agreed. Although he knew nothing would ever be normal between them again. Every time he looked at her, he'd remember holding her in his arms. Every time he spoke to her, he'd remember the taste of her kisses. Despite the fact that he'd halted their lovemaking before the actual act itself could be accomplished, they had crossed a boundary and now could never go back to the innocent relationship they'd once known.

He sat down across from her at the table and gestured to the small stack of tabloids beside her. "I didn't know you went in for literary reading," he teased.

"I don't usually read them, but today you and I were fodder for several articles." She held up one with a headline that read Wild Princess Gets Her Man. A photo similiar to the one that had appeared in the morning paper accompanied the sensational article.

"You shouldn't read that garbage," Gabe said as he helped himself to a piece of the pizza.

Serena shrugged. "I'm going to cut out all the articles and pictures about our wedding and make a scrapbook. In lieu of wedding pictures, these will have to suffice."

"Serena, don't you think that when we get back to Wynborough and the marriage is annulled it would be best if you just put it all behind you?" Gabe asked gently.

"You deal with things your way, Gabriel, and I'll deal with them in my way," she replied. She traced a finger across his face on the front page of one of the papers. "Maybe some day I'll want to show my children the pictures of my first husband." She picked up a piece of pizza.

"You like children, don't you?" he asked, wanting to change the subject.

"I love children." The look in her eyes softened. "For as long as I can remember, I've wanted children of my own. Two…three…maybe half a dozen. The more the merrier.''

"You're good with children," he said, remembering the many times young boys and girls had approached her. She had the patience of a saint with the little ones. It was only one of the qualities that made her a favorite with the public.

Once again they grew silent. Gabe ate his pizza, his head filled with visions of the children Serena would one day have…little girls with flaming hair and dancing dimples or boys with stubborn chins and bright green eyes.

An emotion curiously like grief rose inside Gabe as he realized those children would be hers, but not his. She would have her children with another man, a husband that would be for keeps.

He'd wanted children…a lifetime ago. He'd once dreamed of a little boy who would carry on the Morgan name. Or a little girl who'd wrap her arms around his neck and call him daddy. But he'd put those dreams away, at the same time he'd decided he didn't want love in his life.

He finished his piece of pizza, which had turned to the consistency of sawdust in his mouth. He pushed away from the table, no longer hungry as he thought of Serena marrying another man.

Moving to the window, he stared outside, seeking the emotional distance that had always been his friend, his comfort. He'd always counted on his emotional detachment to keep him sharp, his mind uncluttered. But somehow Serena had destroyed any neutrality he might feel where she was concerned, and that was dangerous.

"Gabe?"

"What?" he asked sharply. He turned back to look at her, wishing his heart felt nothing where she was concerned.

She winced slightly, as if his tone of voice had slapped her. She gestured toward one of the papers opened before her. "There's an article in here about you."

He frowned and walked over to stand just behind her where he could read the headline of the piece. Tragic Past Haunts Bodyguard Groom.

He scanned just enough of the article to realize somebody had done their homework. It was all there, his past as a cop, his marriage to LeAnn and LeAnn's tragic death.

He felt the blood rush from his face, leaving him lightheaded and half-dizzy. "They are nothing but vultures, picking over the pieces of people's lives. I don't know why you read that garbage."

Serena turned around in her chair to look up at him. "Is it true? Were you married before?"

"Read all about it," he said with a touch of bitterness. He pointed to the paper. "They probably have a fact wrong here or there, but what the heck."

Her gaze was somber as she got up from the table and instead sat down on the edge of the sofa. "I'd rather hear it from you, Gabe, than read it in a tabloid."

He wanted to tell her it was none of her business, that it had all happened a long time ago and didn't matter anymore. But there was a part of him that wanted to talk about it, that wanted to explain to Serena what had happened. He needed to make her understand how those events so long ago had changed him and why he would never, ever allow himself to love her as she so wanted to be loved.

He started to sit on the sofa, then changed his mind, needing to walk, to pace while his thoughts carried him back in time. "I met LeAnn when I was working traffic and she sped by me as if begging me to ticket her."

"Did you?" Serena asked.

A ghost of a smile curved his lips as he remembered how LeAnn had flirted and cajoled in an effort to avoid the speeding ticket. "Yeah, I did. I gave her a ticket, then asked her out."

He moved once again to stand at the window and stare outside. "It was a crazy, whirlwind kind of courtship. We only dated for two months, then we got married."

Now, with the perspective of time, Gabe realized he and LeAnn had probably married too quickly and for all the wrong reasons. He had been lonely and LeAnn, reeling from a broken engagement a month before, had been desperate. Despite the odds, despite their differences, they were determined to make the marriage work.

He drew in a deep breath, fast forwarding in his mind to the day it had all ended. "We'd been married about six months on the morning I took her to the bank so she could deposit a check." He turned to look at Serena, the pit of his stomach burning with the memory of that day.

"Gabe...don't." Her gaze was tender, soft with emotion. "If it hurts too much, you don't have to tell me."

Her obvious concern for him and his emotional well-being was almost his undoing. It would be so easy to sweep her up in his arms, carry her into the bedroom and lose himself, his memories and his regrets in her sweet heat.

"No...you need to know," he replied. "You need to understand." Even as he said these words he wondered if she would. He wondered if he even understood all the emotions that had died on the day LeAnn had been killed.

"We'd only been in the bank a minute or two. I was standing near the front door, watching LeAnn as she waited in line." The muscles in his stomach tightened as the memory of that moment grew crystal clear in his mind. "It was a gorgeous summer day and LeAnn was wearing a short dress and sandals."

He shook his head, amazed at the peculiarity of memories a person's brain chose to retain. "She had a blister on one heel. I remember thinking we should stop and get some bandages on the way home."

Pacing back and forth in front of the window, Gabe drew in a deep breath. "I was watching LeAnn, and she was watching the teller when everything went crazy. A voice yelled 'Freeze,' somebody screamed, a gun went off and LeAnn was dead."

"Oh God, Gabe…" Serena stood and took a step toward him, but he stopped her by holding up a hand.

"Apparently a kid, high on drugs, had decided to pull a bank robbery. When he yelled and the teller screamed, he fired the gun. LeAnn was simply an innocent victim who was in the wrong place at the wrong time."

"I don't know what to say. It must have been devastating for you." Serena reached out and tentatively touched his arm, as if unsure how he would react to the physical contact. "You must have loved her very much."

Loved LeAnn? He stared at Serena. What he'd once felt for LeAnn was nothing compared to the emotions Serena had managed to stir inside him.

"Yeah, I loved her, but in the last couple of years, I've come to terms with her loss." The burning in his stomach intensified and he felt the hot press of tears behind his eyelids. Tears he hadn't cried when he'd been a lonely, unwanted child, tears that hadn't been released when LeAnn had died, tears he'd held inside for a lifetime.

He swallowed hard against them, refusing to let them fall. Instead he sought the anger, the self-hatred that had always kept him strong. He stepped away from Serena, so he could no longer feel her comforting touch.

"What I can't forget…what I'll never forget is that I was right there, a cop trained to protect people, and I couldn't even protect my own wife." The words tumbled out of him, a sea of guilt that threatened to drown him. "I was a trained professional. If I hadn't been so busy looking at LeAnn's legs, I would have seen the kid come into the bank. I would have sensed his intent and been able to stop him before anyone got hurt."

"You can't know that," Serena exclaimed. "You can't blame yourself for LeAnn's death."

"I could have stopped it." The words exploded from him. "But caring about her made me stupid and dull. Caring about her made me preoccupied and less perceptive. That's why she's dead. And that's why I'm going to call your father this evening and tell him to send another bodyguard for you. I'm not going to be your bodyguard anymore and I'm not returning to Wynborough with you."

Serena stared at him for a long moment, shocked by his words. Not returning to Wynborough with her? Getting her another bodyguard? Someplace in her mind, she'd known that Gabe would probably try to quit his job as her bodyguard, but she'd been certain before they returned to Wynborough she would be able to change his mind.

She couldn't imagine him not in her life, if not as her husband, then as the man she depended on for her security and protection.

"You can't mean that," she finally spoke into the depth of silence his words had created.

He raked a hand down his jaw, looking exhausted and wrung out. "I do mean it." He slumped into the sofa. Leaning backward he closed his eyes, as if in telling her of his past, he'd used every ounce of energy he possessed.

Serena stared at him, loving him with every ounce of her being. When he'd spoken of his past tragedy, she'd embraced it as her own, her heart aching for him and his loss.

But she refused to embrace the obvious guilt that ate at him. She had a feeling her enemy was not his memories of LeAnn, but rather the culpability he felt because of her death.

Frowning, she tried to climb into his mind, to understand the forces that drove him, the emotions that had dictated the choices he'd made with his life since LeAnn's death.

She sat down next to him. She didn't touch him, knew instinctively he would rebuff any simple touch, any loving caress from her. He leaned forward and buried his face in his hands.

"Gabe, when you took the job as my bodyguard, weren't you seeking redemption?"

He raised his head to look at her, his eyes so dark, so empty, Serena's heart once again constricted with his pain. "Redemption?" He said the word as if it were foreign to his vocabulary. "I wasn't seeking anything," he scoffed. "I needed work. The job fell into my lap so I took it."

"You saved my father's life," she exclaimed.

"A mere accident of fate," he retorted. He averted his gaze from her and instead stared at the surface of the coffee table.

"A mere accident of fate," she repeated with a nod. "Just like LeAnn's death."

Again his gaze found hers, this time burning with intensity, as if the fever of guilt raged hot inside him. "You don't know…you can't know."

She held his gaze, unflinching. "I know this… I've always felt completely safe with you. I've always trusted that you would protect me. I've never had a moment of doubt about that."

He sighed and some of the intensity of his gaze lessened. "I never had a moment of doubt until now, but now I know it's time to move on. I can't guarantee your safety any longer."

"Why? What's changed?" Serena asked desperately. "You haven't doubted yourself before today…before this moment. What's happened to change you?"

He stood, his features ravaged with torment. "I'm out of control where you are concerned," he yelled angrily. "I want you, and it's eating me alive. I can't keep my mind on anything else. Don't you understand, I'm a security risk now." He turned away from her. "I need a little time alone," he said and stalked to his bedroom.

Serena watched him disappear, stared at the door he closed behind him. He wanted her. He couldn't think of anything else. Her heart sang with the knowledge. And she knew beneath his desire for her was love. He loved her.

The joy that filled her heart was short-lived as she stared at the bedroom door. What good did it do for her to know he loved her, for him to want her beyond reason, if he didn't intend to spend his life with her? If he continued to fight against what was in his heart?

She had to figure out a way to get through to him, to ease the guilt that had eaten at him for far too long and now threatened to destroy any hope they had for a future together. But how? How could she make him forgive himself? How could she make him not afraid to accept their love for each other?

The afternoon brought her no answers. Gabe stayed in his room until dinnertime. When he finally came out, he appeared completely in control and coolly detached from her. "Why don't we go out for dinner," he suggested. "I think we both could use a little fresh air."

"Okay," she agreed, disheartened by the hours that had brought no easy answers.

They found a quiet little Italian restaurant not far from their hotel and were led to a secluded table in the rear by a friendly hostess.

They had not spoken on the short walk to the restaurant. It was as if both of them were afraid to say anything that might shatter the tenuous calm between them.

"It smells wonderful in here," Gabe said as he opened his menu. "Are you hungry?" He looked at her and in his eyes she saw his need to keep things normal, devoid of the emotions that had torn them apart earlier.

"A little," she replied. The light from the candle in the center of the table played on her wedding ring and Serena felt a helpless sense of defeat.

Was she wrong in believing that he loved her? Maybe she was fooling herself. Maybe what he felt for her had nothing to do with love. Was it only lust that made him want her, a lust with no basis for forever?

They ordered their meal, then once again silence grew between them. Serena sipped a glass of wine, trying to keep her gaze averted from Gabe. It hurt too much to look at him, to remember the heat of his kisses, the feel of his hands caressing her body. It hurt too much to know he intended to walk away from her rather than risk loving again.

"Serena? I'm sorry."

She looked at him then, saw the sorrow that deepened the hue of his eyes. She shrugged and took another sip of her wine. "Don't be sorry for me, Gabe. Be sorry for yourself. You're the only loser in this whole thing."

He flushed slightly and averted his gaze from hers. "Then that makes you the winner, and that's all that's important to me."

Anger rose inside her. "That's where you're wrong." She bit off what she was about to say as the waitress appeared at their table with their dinners.

"Here we are. Lasagna for the lady and spaghetti and meatballs for the gentleman," she said with a perky smile. "A meal fit for royalty." The waitress giggled with excitement. "I saw in the paper where you two got married and I just wanted to extend my congratulations." She giggled again and pulled a slip of paper and a pen from her apron. "Would you mind...could I have your autographs?"

"Of course," Serena replied with the graciousness she'd been taught from the cradle. She signed the paper, then pushed it to Gabe, who signed it as well.

"Thanks so much," the waitress gushed. "I've never met a prince and princess before."

"But I'm not—" Gabe began.

"You're welcome," Serena interrupted him.

"Enjoy your meal. Just let me know if you need anything." With another giggle, the waitress left their table.

"She'll be disappointed when she realizes I'm not a prince, but just your bodyguard," Gabe observed.

Just your bodyguard. How easily he discounted everything he'd become to her.

"She'll probably find that autograph worth a lot of money some day," Serena said. "After all, it will be the only autograph of a princess and her husband during the brief time they were married."

Once again silence prevailed. The low sounds of mood music floating in the air did nothing to break the stifling quiet as they ate.

As Serena shot Gabe surreptitious glances, she realized she'd been wrong when she'd thought to keep him as her bodyguard. If she couldn't have him in her life as her husband, it was better that he not be in her life in any capacity.

She would die a little bit each day seeing him, having him near, having him protect her as his job, as his duty, yet knowing there would never be a future for the two of them.

They had finished their meal and had ordered coffee when Gabe once again spoke. "I called your father this afternoon and told him you were ready to return home but needed a new bodyguard to escort you. He's sending a man named Lance Grayson. Grayson will be here first thing in the morning and your flight home leaves at noon."

"Tomorrow?" she echoed in dismay. Too fast. It was all happening too fast. She had hoped for more time…time to figure out what to do, time to figure out how to change Gabe's mind, to help him accept the love she knew that resided in his heart.

Up until this moment, she'd held on to her pride, but she felt that pride flitting away as desperation grew stronger. She wanted to give him one last chance, to try one final time to change his mind, but not here in the restaurant.

"I don't really want coffee," she said. "I need to get back to the hotel and start packing if I'm returning home tomorrow."

"Okay," he agreed. "I can always order up some coffee from room service." He paid their tab and they left the restaurant.

Outside, the lights of Las Vegas lit the night as if the sun had never set. But night was upon them, and Serena knew it was her last night with Gabe. In the morning a new bodyguard would arrive, and he and Serena would return to Wynborough.

She looked at Gabe as they entered the lobby of

their hotel. "What are your plans? If you aren't going back to Wynborough, where are you going?"

As they got into the elevator, he punched the button for their floor. "I'm going back to Kansas City." He leaned against the elevator wall. "I'm not sure what I'm going to do there, but that's where I'm going. My flight leaves tomorrow about the same time yours does."

The elevator halted and the two of them got off and entered their suite. Serena turned to Gabe just inside the door. "Gabe…I can't make you forgive yourself for whatever responsibility you feel about LeAnn's death. All I can tell you is that I love you with all my heart, with all my soul."

She had expected him to back away from her, but he didn't. Instead, he reached out and ran a finger down her cheek, his touch so sweet, so achingly tender, it caused tears of frustration to spring to her eyes.

"Serena, you're so young, such an innocent. You deserve much better than what I can offer you. Besides—" he allowed his finger to linger on her chin "—what do you know about love? It's only natural you believe yourself in love with me because I've been the only consistent man in your life."

"You pompous ass," Serena exploded as she shoved his hand away from her face. Anger swept through her as she glared at him. "How dare you."

"Serena," he protested with surprise.

"How dare you tell me what you think I really feel for you," she said. "I know what's in my heart, Gabriel Morgan, and it's real love, true love. I love you despite the fact that you're overbearing and arrogant. I love how I feel when I'm with you, how you make me want to be a better woman. I'm not confused about my feelings for you."

The words tumbled from her, one after another, and when tears stung her eyes, she angrily swiped them away. "You act like you're the only person in the world who has suffered loss, like tragedy has never touched another person but you." He opened his mouth, apparently to protest, but Serena gave him no opportunity.

"Twenty-nine years ago, my brother was kidnapped...a terrible tragedy that haunts my parents still. Don't you think my mother blamed herself, wondered what she could have done differently to keep James safe? Yet she didn't stop living, stop loving. She went on to have four more children when she could have allowed that tragedy to keep her childless forever."

Gabe moved away from her and sank to the sofa. But Serena wasn't finished yet. Emotion still pressed in her chest, myriad emotions of anger and bitterness, of need and grief, and the desperation of a woman in love.

"How arrogant you are to accept full responsibility for LeAnn's death. How egotistical of you to believe you're godlike and had the ultimate power to save her. Some things are just meant to be. They're out of our control and there's nothing to be done about it but have the courage to go on." She paused, half-breathless from the expulsion of words.

"Are you through?" he asked, his voice cool, his eyes blank...emotionless.

She drew a deep breath and shoved her hair behind her ears. "No, I'm not through," she said, her voice softer, more controlled. She sat on the opposite end of the sofa, her gaze not leaving him.

For a moment she couldn't continue speaking. She was so filled with her love for him, it made speech momentarily impossible. She realized she'd loved Gabe since the first day he'd become her bodyguard. She'd tried to tell herself it was a silly crush, an impossible case of puppy love, but that crush had transformed, and what she felt for him now was the mature, enduring love of a lifetime.

"Gabe, I love you, and nothing is ever going to change that." He stiffened slightly as if in defense. "Just tell me one thing...do you love me?"

The words hung in the air, and Serena's heart resonated with frantic thuds as she waited for his answer. If he told her he didn't love her, then she'd know it was truly over and she wouldn't fight the annulment. If he told her he loved her, then all bets were off and she would do her best to make him learn to trust in that love.

"Serena..." He averted his gaze from hers. "I've made up my mind about what I'm doing and—"

"Just answer the question, Gabe," she interrupted, feeling as if she might scream if he didn't tell her now.

"I told you before that I want you. I want to make love to you. I desire you." He stood and looked at her once again. "I also told you that I didn't have a heart." His voice was low, soft. "And without a heart there can be no love."

Serena's heart seemed to stop beating altogether. He doesn't love you, a voice cried in her head. You were wrong about him, wrong to believe that he did love you.

She stood, her legs wobbly and her head swimming with tears she refused to release. "Well, then that's that. It's time for me to pack for the trip home tomorrow." She was glad her voice sounded normal.

She walked to her bedroom door, then turned back to gaze at him. "You know, LeAnn's death wasn't the real tragedy." She swallowed hard, then continued, "And you not loving me isn't really the ultimate tragedy. The real tragedy in all of this is that you died on that day in the bank. As long as you keep yourself closed off from love, you won't really live. You're a walking dead man, Gabriel, and you don't even know it." She turned and went into her room and closed the door behind her.

Chapter Ten

When a knock fell on the door at ten the next morning, Gabe assumed it was the new bodyguard arriving. He was surprised to open the door and find an older, balding man in a suit and tie. The man held out a badge.

"Lieutenant Breckenridge."

Gabe greeted the man with a handshake and invited him inside. "Nice to meet you, sir."

"You, too, Mr. Morgan," Breckenridge returned.

"I'd like to thank you for your help in finding Betty Jo Parker. Princess Serena was pleased by the cooperation of your department."

"No problem." The lieutenant shifted from one foot to the other, obviously ill at ease. "Actually, I'm here about another matter."

Gabe looked at him curiously. What other matter could a member of the Las Vegas police department have with them?

"Actually, the captain sent me over as a sort of courtesy call. We're a tourist city, and we like to think we look after the tourists who come here. And that means we try to keep tabs on the nefarious characters who call Las Vegas home." He frowned and scratched his balding head. "The captain was quite upset when I told him about your phone call to me checking up on Avery Kintell."

Gabe shot a quick glance to Serena's bedroom door which was open, but he saw no sign of Serena. He gestured for the lieutenant to step out into the hallway, then he pulled the suite door closed behind him.

"I can tell you Avery Kintell is a dead issue. In any case, the princess and I are leaving Las Vegas today so Avery Kintell will have to find another mark."

Lieutenant Breckenridge nodded. "Good. The man is slippery as a snake and we try to keep tabs on him. Unfortunately, legally we can't do much about him."

"Tell your captain we appreciate his concern."

Breckenridge nodded. "We hope you and the princess will come back to visit again sometime."

The two men said their goodbyes, then Gabe returned to the suite. He was grateful there was still no sign of Serena. The last thing he wanted her to find out was that Avery had only been interested in her because she was a wealthy princess. Gabe knew that information would only serve to hurt Serena.

He poured himself a cup of coffee from the room service cart, then sat down at the table.

His eyes felt gritty with lack of sleep. All night long he'd tossed and turned, Serena's words echoing over and over again in his mind. He knew what he was doing was right. He knew she would be better off married to a prince, a duke, an earl. What he hadn't realized was that leaving her would be so difficult.

Already he dreaded the ride to the airport, dreaded the goodbyes they would say to each other as she got on her plane and he took off for his flight.

He'd only seen her once that morning, when she'd brought her suitcase from her bedroom and placed it by the front door.

She hadn't spoken to him, but had returned immediately to her room. No chatter, no smile, no nothing. The heart he had professed not to have ached with the absence of her generous warmth, her natural vitality.

He sighed in relief as another knock sounded at the door. Surely that would be the new bodyguard. He opened the door to reveal a tall, well-built man with black hair and cool gray eyes. "Gabriel Morgan?" the man inquired.

Gabe nodded. "And you must be Lance Grayson." He gestured the man inside. "Nice suit," he commented. Lance wore an exact copy of the navy suit Gabe wore.

Grayson smiled ruefully. "And the tailor told me it was one of a kind."

Gabe laughed despite the sick feeling in the pit of his stomach. Not only good-looking, but with a sense of humor as well. Why hadn't King Phillip sent somebody older…less handsome? Lance looked to be in his early thirties, just the right age for a princess looking for love.

"Would you like a cup of coffee? We have a few minutes before we need to get to the airport."

"Sounds great," Lance agreed.

Gabe poured him a cup, then the two sat at the table. Lance remained rigid, not relaxing despite the fact he was seated.

Gabe noted that his gaze swiftly darted around the room. The sign of a man automatically checking out the room's security, making mental notes of entrances and exits.

He should feel glad that Serena was going to be in good hands, but he found nothing vaguely similar to gladness in his heart.

Both men turned as Serena stepped from her room. Dressed in a pair of jeans and a vibrant yellow blouse, with her hair wild and curly down her back, she filled the room with her presence, like a shining beacon on the darkest night.

Gabe's heart, the heart he insisted he didn't have, did a peculiar lurch. He stood, as did Lance. "Serena, this is Lance Grayson."

"Ah yes, the new warden." She shook his hand, then gestured them both back to their seats. "Do I have time for a quick cup of coffee?" she asked.

Gabe looked at his watch. "We have about fifteen minutes before we need to get to the airport."

She poured herself a cup, then joined them at the table. "My parents are well?" she asked Lance.

"Yes, and eager for you to come home," Lance replied.

Serena studiously ignored Gabe as she made small talk with the new bodyguard. So much for her love, he thought, growing more certain that he was doing the right thing.

She'd apparently managed to get over loving him through the long hours of last night. She appeared cheerful as she talked to Lance, with no shadows of unhappiness or misery darkening the emerald hue of her eyes.

Young love, he thought ruefully. Deeply felt, quickly forgotten. Yes, it was best that he leave her. She had obviously mistaken trust and familiarity for love.

Serena was a survivor, with a joy for life and a romantic soul that would make her quickly forget the bodyguard she'd thought she loved.

They finished their coffee, then Gabe carried their bags to the awaiting car and they headed for the airport.

All too quickly they were not only at the airport but at the gate where Serena and Lance would catch their flight. It was time to say goodbye.

"I'll stay in touch with your father," Gabe said. "In case there are papers I need to sign or whatever." The animation that Serena had exhibited for the last hour in Lance's presence was gone, and a deep sadness darkened her eyes as she faced him.

Gabe gazed at Lance, who stood nearby, looking alert and attentive to the crowd. "You're in good hands with Lance. He appears to be quite competent.'' He forced a smile. ''Your father would have sent only the best.'' He drew a deep breath. ''So, I guess this is goodbye.''

She nodded, then before he could guess her intent, she wrapped her arms around his neck and pressed herself against him as her lips sought his.

He had a moment to think about stopping the kiss, but the moment vanished the instant her lips touched his. He drank of her, relishing the sweet fire of the kiss, the bewitching warmth of her body intimately pressed against his.

Wrapping his arms around her, he tangled his hands in her fresh-scented hair, then caressed down her back, losing himself in the kiss, in her.

The kiss seemed to last both an eternity and a mere split second. It was far too long, and achingly short. When he finally ended the kiss, he murmured a goodbye, then turned and walked away.

He didn't look back. He couldn't. Funny, how a man who didn't have a heart could feel so utterly broken inside.

He went directly to the gate where his flight would be boarding within the next few minutes. Slumping into a chair, he tried to shove all thoughts of Serena from his mind.

Serena, in the pretty white suit when he'd married her. Serena, her head thrown back in laughter, eyes sparkling like expensive gems. Serena, in that damnable sexy nightgown, stretching languidly with her hair all tousled around her head.

Visions like snapshots exploding in his mind refused to let him forget a moment, a second of his time with her. Clad in her snow jacket, attempting to sneak out of the Aspen house. Legs and arms tangled with his and the morning sunlight radiant on her face.

It hadn't just been about desire, he finally acknowledged to himself. He'd been fooling himself, believing that desire was all he felt for her.

It had been about love. He loved her as he'd never loved before and had a feeling he never would again, but he knew his decision to walk away from her was the right one.

He didn't know how long he sat there, playing and replaying moments with Serena in his mind, telling himself over and over again that her love hadn't been real, would never have lasted. His thoughts were finally interrupted by a monotone voice over the loud speaker announcing the boarding of his plane. He got in line with the other travelers.

"Morgan!"

He turned to see Lance Grayson hurrying toward him, a tense look on the man's face and no Serena in sight.

"Don't tell me," Gabe said as Lance approached. "She gave you the slip."

Lance nodded curtly. "She went into a gift shop and disappeared."

It's not your problem, a little voice whispered in Gabe's head. It's Grayson's problem. You are no longer responsible. His head said one thing, but his heart said another.

"Damn," Gabe said succinctly and raked a hand through his hair. "I should have warned you that she is like Houdini when it comes to making great escapes.''

Gabe picked up his bag and slung it over his shoulder. ''Come on, let's go find her. Surely one slip of a woman can't evade the pursuit of two trained professionals.''

Together, the two men walked back toward the gift shop where she had disappeared. While Lance checked the right side of the concourse, Gabe checked the left. Where would she have gone? Why in the heck would she ditch Grayson just before her flight?

Gabe's head raced with questions. As always, he found it impossible to second-guess Serena. They went into the gift shop where she had disappeared and discovered a side door inside that led to rest rooms, then back to the terminal.

Shouting a warning, Gabe went into the ladies' rest room, startling the sole occupant, an elderly woman washing her hands at the sink. He exited and caught up with Lance.

''This has never happened to me before,'' he said to Gabe, a frown creasing his brow. ''What if she didn't just sneak away? What if somebody has kidnapped her?''

''Then heaven help them...they'll have their hands full,'' Gabe returned dryly, but the same fear had already knocked on his heart.

Where in the hell was Serena?

Serena boarded the plane and found her seat. Sinking into it, she swept the silly hat she'd bought in the gift shop off her head. With her hair tucked up, she'd managed to pass within twenty yards of Gabe and Lance without them spotting her.

Losing Lance had been easy. She had a feeling the man had never had a person he was guarding actively try to get away from him. He hadn't been expecting her to ditch him, and so he hadn't taken the kind of precautions Gabe would have. Gabe never would have allowed her to enter a store alone. Gabe never would have allowed her out of his sight for an instant.

Gabe. Her heart cried his name as she stuffed the hat beneath her seat, then leaned back. Her heart thudded rapidly, beating the rhythm of anticipation and uncertainty.

She closed her eyes, hoping she wasn't making the biggest mistake of her life.

There were two things that had happened to prompt her action. First, she'd been shocked when she'd overheard what Lieutenant Breckenridge had said about Avery Kintell. She'd been completely blown away when she realized Gabe had known about Avery and hadn't told her.

She'd spent the morning contemplating what it meant. Gabe had known Avery was probably only after her because she was Princess Serena. He could have told her that at any time, but he'd chosen not to.

Why? The only answer that made sense was that he hadn't wanted to hurt her. And a man who didn't care about a woman didn't do things to spare her feelings. It would have been so much easier to tell her about Avery than to marry her.

The second thing that had made her realize what she wanted—needed to do—was their kiss goodbye. Gabe's kiss had said to her all the things he'd been unable to verbalize.

The kiss had spoken of love.

He loved her. Serena knew she wasn't wrong. She prayed she wasn't wrong. She'd taken her ticket and turned it in for one on the same flight as Gabe's to Kansas City. She'd finagled and cajoled to get assigned the seat next to his. Now all she had to do was wait for him to board…wait to see if he surrendered himself to love…or threw her off the plane.

As the minutes ticked by, her heartbeat raced frantically and she wondered if it were possible for a twenty-one-year-old woman to have a heart attack.

Where was he? Why hadn't he boarded yet? She twisted her wedding band around and around her finger, a band she hoped she never had to remove.

Passengers filled the aisles, storing overhead bags, finding their seats. Doubts plagued her mind. What if she was wrong about his love? When she'd asked him if he loved her the night before, he'd not been able to tell her he did. But he hadn't said he didn't love her.

She closed her eyes, praying she'd been right, praying that she hadn't made a huge mistake.

"Going somewhere?"

The deep, sweetly familiar voice washed over her and she opened her eyes to see Gabe. His eyes burned with anger and his features were taut with tension.

She raised her chin and eyed him defiantly. "As a matter of fact, I am. I'm going to Kansas City with my husband. That's what married people do...they travel together."

"Your disappearance act gave Lance a near heart attack." Gabe sank into the seat next to her to get out of the way of other passengers.

She frowned, chagrined that she'd worried Lance. "I'm sorry I scared him. He seems very nice. But a woman has to do what a woman has to do. And this woman intends to follow her husband wherever he goes...to be with him whatever he does."

Some of the anger left Gabe's eyes, but the tension in his face didn't dissipate. "You crazy fool."

She flushed. "I'm not crazy. I'm willful and spoiled and I know exactly what I want and I don't intend to settle for anything less."

A tic appeared in Gabe's jaw. "You're supposed to be on a plane back to Wynborough with Lance."

She ignored him, intent on saying what was in her heart. "Let me tell you exactly what it is that I want. I want you. I want to be Mrs. Gabriel Morgan for the rest of my life. I want to have your children. I want to go to sleep at night and wake up in the morning with your arms around me. I want to dream with you, then work to build those dreams. I want to take your hopes and make them mine. I want to share all the big and little things that life brings...the joys and the sorrows."

She placed her hand on his jaw, where that muscle

ticked erratically. "I want to give you all the hugs you never had as a child, give you all the days of joy that were stolen from you. Gabriel Morgan, I love you and I intend to stick to you like tread on a tire."

At some point during her monologue, his muscle had stopped throbbing and his gaze had softened. "You make it sound like I have no choice in the matter," he said, a touch of indulgent amusement in his voice.

"You don't," she said with a conviction she didn't feel. "I've made up my mind. We belong together, and that's that." She held her breath, waiting for him to say something…anything.

The certainty she'd managed to keep in her voice wasn't in her heart. She still didn't know if he was going to carry her off the plane and out of his life.

"Gabriel, if you're worried that loving me will make you less sharp, less competent as my bodyguard, then quit your job as my bodyguard…don't quit being my husband."

He stood suddenly. Leaning over, he scooped her from her seat and into his arms. "Gabe…please…" Tears sprang to her eyes as he carried her down the narrow aisle and off the plane.

"Please, don't put me on that plane to Wynborough unless you intend to be on it with me," she cried.

"You are the most irritating, aggravating woman I've ever known," Gabe said as he put her down. He held her shoulders. "And I'm not putting you on the plane to Wynborough. I'm not about to spend my first night as a real married man on an airplane."

"A real married man?" Serena stared at him intently, her tears disappearing as a small flame of hope warmed her heart. "Gabe?"

He gazed at her, a tenderness she'd never seen on his face. "You said a lot of things to me last night that for the first time made sense." He dropped his hands from her shoulders. "I will always feel a certain amount of responsibility for LeAnn's death, but I can live with it. What I can't do is live without you."

He placed a finger against her lips as she opened them to speak. "I want to live every moment of every day with you. I want to be beside you when you give birth. I want to share in the celebration when James is found...and he will be found."

Again, his hands went to her shoulders, his touch gentle as his thumbs made tiny circles over her collarbone. "You asked me a question last night and I sidestepped it. Now I need to answer it. Yes, I love you." He smiled, a smile that transformed her hope into promise. "I love you madly, passionately." His voice trembled with emotion. "When Lance came running up to me and told me you were gone, I realized I didn't want to live without you. And when we couldn't find you, I thought I was going to lose my mind. I got on that plane hoping, praying you'd be there, hoping and praying that for once in my life I guessed what you intended to do."

"Oh, Gabe." She melted into his arms and their lips met in a fiery kiss that spoke of hunger, and need, and the incredible love that had blossomed between them.

For the first time in her life, Serena felt that she was finally where she belonged, in his arms with his words of love ringing in her ear.

"So, if we aren't going to Wynborough and we aren't going to Kansas City, where are we going?" she asked when their kiss had finally ended.

"We're going back to the hotel, and we're going to spend the night making love, and building dreams and planning our future because..."

"That's what married people do," she finished for him.

He laughed and hugged her close. "Yes, my love. That's what married people do."

Epilogue

Serena awoke to the early morning sun streaming through the hotel suite window and Gabe's warm, muscular body snuggled against her own. For a long moment she remained unmoving, eyes closed, allowing memories of the night before to play through her mind.

It had been a night beyond her imagination. In her wildest dreams, she'd never envisioned that making love with Gabe would be so exciting and wonderful. She'd never fantasized that the man she'd married, the bodyguard she adored, would be such a tender, patient lover.

Even now, remembering the heat of his kisses, the magic of his touch, her entire body tingled with pleasure, and the anticipation of making love with Gabe again.

She opened her eyes and smiled as she saw he

still slept soundly. He was finally, truly hers, and never had she loved anything or anyone so completely.

For a moment she remained still, watching him sleep, her heart filled with the utter pureness of her love. The sunlight danced across his face, emphasizing the length of his dark lashes, the sensual curve of his mouth.

She thought about waking him up, then reconsidered. He was probably exhausted. They had made love for more than half the night. She'd let him sleep and order a breakfast fit for a king.

Carefully, she eased away from him and out of bed. In the adjoining bathroom she washed, brushed the tangles from her hair, then slipped on a dressing gown. She left the bathroom on tip-toes and headed for the door to the next room.

"Going somewhere?"

His deep voice sent a shiver of delight racing up her spine. She turned and faced him, her breath catching as he raised up on his elbows and the sheet fell away from his naked chest.

"I'm hungry," she said, wondering how it was possible that she felt shy after the night they had shared.

"So am I." His eyes glittered wickedly and a sweet rush of heat suffused Serena.

"I...I thought I'd order room service." Her mouth was suddenly dry as her internal temperature seemed to rise.

"They don't serve what I'm hungry for." His voice was deep and husky.

"And what are you hungry for?" she asked breathlessly.

"My wife."

Her eyes widened as he got out of bed, splendid in his nakedness. When he reached her, he scooped her up in his arms. "It seems I'm always chasing after you," he said as he carried her back to the bed.

She placed a hand on his cheek and smiled teasingly. "I promise I'll never run so fast that you can't catch me."

He laughed and together they tumbled to the bed. His laughter lasted only a moment, for his lips found hers in a fiery kiss that left them both breathless.

Serena was on her back, and her heart pounded furiously in her chest as his fingers danced across the dainty buttons of her dressing gown.

"Tell me, my beautiful, sweet Serena. What are you hungry for?" Her breath caught in her throat as his hand skimmed across the top of her aching breasts. "Omelets?" He unbuttoned the first button. "Pancakes?" The second button came undone. "Waffles?" With the release of the third button, the sides of the gown fell away, exposing her nakedness to his hungry gaze.

"You," she whispered fervently. "Always and only you, Gabe."

Again his mouth found hers, kissing her with a hunger she felt deep inside her. It was a deep kiss that stirred her to dizzying heights, and when his hands cupped her breasts, his thumbs teasing the swollen peaks, she moaned his name.

He pulled his mouth from hers, his eyes blazing

with flames of desire. "Do you have any idea how much I love you, Serena Morgan?"

She thrilled at the name...his name, now her own. "Show me," she whispered. "Show me how much you love me."

And he did. He made love to her with a passion tempered by tenderness, a desire born of their love. She matched him touch for touch, caress for caress, moving with him as tiny little cries of pleasure escaped her.

He loved her until she was incapable of a coherent thought, until there was nothing else in the world but him and their escalating need for each other.

When finally their need was spent, they remained in each other's arms, facing each other and gazing into each other's eyes.

"Will it always be like this?" she asked, her fingers teasing the hair on his chest.

"Like what?" He used his index finger to stroke down the side of her cheek.

"So...so...wonderful." She frowned, aware that the word was inadequate to describe what they'd just shared.

He smiled, an indulgent smile that not only curved his lips, but lit the darkness of his eyes. "Always."

"And will you love me madly, passionately, forever?"

"Forever." The word was a promise she knew she could count on.

The shrill ring of the telephone on the bedside stand broke the moment. "It must be one of my sisters," Serena said, then rolled over and grabbed the receiver. "Hi, Elizabeth," she greeted the caller.

Gabe watched his wife as she talked, loving the expressions that swept over her face, loving the way her hair sparkled like flames in the sunshine. He paid no attention to the conversation, preferring to indulge himself by nibbling the sweetness of her shoulder.

He couldn't believe this woman, this sassy, sexy unpredictable woman was his. She'd healed his spirit, restored his dreams and he knew his future with her would be an exciting adventure of laughter and love.

She hung up the phone, an endearing frown wrinkling her forehead. "Problems?" he asked.

"I can't believe Elizabeth is about five months pregnant and won't say who the father is. I told her she should at least tell the baby's father."

"It's not your problem," he said, once again kissing her shoulder.

"She's attending a fund-raiser in Phoenix, then she's going to try to find Sam Flynn." Serena looked at him. "It's possible Sam Flynn is my brother, James. Maybe we should—"

"Forget it," Gabe exclaimed. "I see the wheels turning in your head and that always means trouble. We are not going to Phoenix. Elizabeth is perfectly capable of finding this Sam Flynn."

"But..."

Whatever she was about to say was lost beneath the kiss Gabe pressed onto her lips. He knew with certainty he'd never get tired of the taste of her, the feel of her body against his.

"If we aren't going to Phoenix, then what are we going to do?" she asked when the kiss finally ended.

"We're returning to Wynborough." He stroked the fire of her hair, loved the impish gleam in her brilliant eyes. "When we get there, we'll find ourselves a beautiful little cottage and we'll make lots of babies."

"Hmmm." She snuggled against him. "That sounds wonderful. I love you, Gabriel Morgan."

"And I love you, Princess Serena." Gabe's heart filled to overflowing as he once again kissed his princess, his wife.

*   *   *   *   *

Turn the page for a sneak preview
of the next magnificent
ROYALLY WED title,

THE PREGNANT PRINCESS

Princess Elizabeth's story!

by rising star

Anne Marie Winston

on sale in January 2000
in Silhouette Desire....

Hello, my sweet one. Perhaps we'll meet your daddy today. As the waiter rushed off with her dinner order, Elizabeth Wyndham felt a slight but very real movement pushing at the wall of her womb. Discreetly covering her abdomen with one hand, she patted the small bulge beneath her fashionable loose-fitting pants and tunic top.

Oh, how she hoped she would be able to locate the man with whom she'd shared such a wonderful night of loving months before in Wynborough. He'd left behind a business card, letting her know where she could find him. Thorton Design and Construction, Phoenix, Arizona.

She'd hoped he would come back for her and, of course, that was still possible. In fact, she was sure he would, since she was absolutely positive he had felt the extraordinary bond between them as strongly as she had.

But she couldn't wait much longer. He didn't know she was on a rather urgent schedule now. Soon she was going to have to tell her parents about her pregnancy.

When she'd had the opportunity to come to the States with her three sisters to search for their long-lost brother, she'd seized the chance. It had been the sheerest good fortune that their search had led them to Hope, Arizona, to a foster home where their kidnapped brother was believed to have been brought nearly thirty years ago. And even better fortune that Catalina, where she was going to interview a man who might be that brother, was but a few hours' drive from her current location, providing her with a perfectly good reason to stay in Phoenix...and to find her Prince Charming from the charity ball.

Oh, he'd been so handsome, so wonderful. From the moment their eyes had met across the crowded ballroom, she'd known he was destined to be some-one very special in her life. They'd danced and drank champagne, and within hours she'd fallen head over heels in love. No, that wasn't true. She'd fallen in love the moment their eyes had made the connection across the ballroom. And she was fairly sure her lover had felt the same way.

Rafe. Her mind moved tenderly over the single stern syllable.

The memory of that perfect evening still made her smile. She'd talked Serena into telling the guards that she'd already retired to her rooms for the night. And then Elizabeth had led Rafe to the little octagonal pavilion at the far end of the formal gardens.

The little glass-walled house was furnished with simple chaise lounges for whiling away long, lazy summer afternoons. One of those lounges would forever linger in her memory. Rafe had kissed her until she thought she might die of pleasure, and then he'd gently drawn her down onto the chaise and—

"Take me to the princess's table." The brusque, masculine voice penetrated her daydreaming.

"The princess is dining alone, sir. I don't think—"

Her heart already had begun to beat frantically as she recognized Rafe's voice. She'd planned on visiting him tomorrow, hadn't expected to see him so soon! She half stood, and her napkin slid to the floor.

But she didn't notice. All her attention was riveted on the man standing in the archway of the dining room.

The man whose steady gaze compelled her not to look away, as memories of their hours together sizzled through the air between them.

His eyes were a dark, dangerous blue. The last time they'd met, those blue eyes had been warm with desire. Right now, they were flashing with a combination of puzzlement, wariness, and what she was pretty sure was a touch of anger.

"Never mind. I see her." He started forward, completely ignoring the fluttering waiters hovering around him.

"But...sir! You are hardly dressed for—sir! A tie and jacket are required in the dining room...."

As her broad-shouldered lover advanced toward her alcove, she took a deep breath, ignoring the sudden doubts that fluttered through her brain.

He'd be happy to see her. Of course he would. And he'd be as thrilled about the baby as she was.

The baby! Some protective maternal mechanism prompted her to resume her seat. Quickly, she reached for her napkin and draped it over her lap, pulling loose the folds of her tunic so that the barely noticeable swell of her abdomen was hidden. She didn't question the instinct that told her this was not the time to tell him of his coming fatherhood. That could come later. After they'd gotten to know each other better.

The thought made her feel hot all over. Raising her chin, she let the warmth of her feelings show in her eyes as she smiled at the man approaching her table.

The man whose set, unsmiling face didn't offer anything remotely resembling the welcome she'd prayed he would extend.

He was huge. That was the first thing that registered now that she'd gotten over the surprise of seeing him so unexpectedly. Oh, she'd remembered he was big, but the man striding toward her, wearing a white T-shirt, faded jeans cinched by a snug leather belt with a heavy silver buckle and dust-covered work boots was simply enormous. But as she focused on his face, she knew he was indeed the man to whom she'd given her heart and so much more five months ago.

"How did you find me?"

Whatever she'd expected, that wasn't part of any greeting she could imagine. "Your card," she said, raising her hands helplessly. "The one you left for me."

"I didn't leave you any card."

"Don't you remember? It was on the chaise when I—" She halted in sudden acute embarrassment.

Then the meaning of his denial struck her. He hadn't meant to leave his card behind. Hadn't intended that she ever know who he was. The idea was crushing, and for a long moment she couldn't even force herself to form words. Finally, lifting her chin, she put on the most regal expression she possessed. "Apparently I was wrong to assume you intended me to look you up if I was in the States," she said in a cool, smooth voice. "I apologize."

"I told my father years ago I wouldn't marry any of you."

Her face reflected her bewilderment. "What are you talking about?"

"About an arranged marriage. To one of the princesses." He crossed his arms and scowled at her. "To *you*." He stabbed a finger in her direction. The move made his muscular arms bulge and the shirt strained at its seams across his chest. He still stood over her and if he wanted to intimidate her, he was doing a darn good job.

But she wasn't going to let him cow her. Never mind that her hopeful heart was breaking into a thousand little pieces. Thank heavens she hadn't had a chance to share any of her foolish dreams with him. "I didn't come here to marry you," she said in a slow, measured tone that barely eked past the lump in her throat.

His expression darkened even more. If that was possible. Slowly, he uncrossed his arms and leaned forward across the table, planting his big palms flat on the surface. He was invading her space and she forced herself not to scoot backward away from him.

"I am not amused by your little act," he said through his teeth. "If you came here hoping to take me back to Wynborough like some kind of damned trophy, you can think again, Princess."

It was so far from the passionate greeting she'd imagined all these months like a stupid fool that she had to fight the tears that welled up. What was wrong with him? She hadn't done anything to make him so angry.

"I didn't come here to take you anywhere," she said, swallowing hard to keep the sobs at bay. "I am here on another matter entirely—although I did wish to talk to you."

There was a tense silence. The man who'd been her lover didn't move a muscle for a long second. She felt a tear escape and trickle down her cheek, but she didn't even raise a hand to brush it away. "Who are you, anyway?" she asked in a shaky voice.

He smiled. A wide baring of perfect white teeth that somehow was more of a threat than a pleasantry. Reaching across the table, he picked up her small, fisted hand and bowed low over it. "Rafael Michelangelo Edward Thorton, eldest son of the Grand Duke of Thortonburg, at your service," he said. "As if you didn't know. Expect me for dinner in your suite tomorrow evening at seven."

Before she could pull away, he pressed an overly courteous kiss to the back of her hand, his gaze holding hers. Then his lips compressed into a thin line as he straightened abruptly. "And be ready to answer my questions this time, Princess."

If you enjoyed what you just read,
then we've got an offer you can't resist!

Take 2 bestselling love stories FREE!

Plus get a FREE surprise gift!

Clip this page and mail it to Silhouette Reader Service™

IN U.S.A.	IN CANADA
3010 Walden Ave.	P.O. Box 609
P.O. Box 1867	Fort Erie, Ontario
Buffalo, N.Y. 14240-1867	L2A 5X3

YES! Please send me 2 free Silhouette Romance® novels and my free surprise gift. Then send me 6 brand-new novels every month, which I will receive months before they're available in stores. In the U.S.A., bill me at the bargain price of $2.90 plus 25¢ delivery per book and applicable sales tax, if any*. In Canada, bill me at the bargain price of $3.25 plus 25¢ delivery per book and applicable taxes**. That's the complete price and a savings of over 10% off the cover prices—what a great deal! I understand that accepting the 2 free books and gift places me under no obligation ever to buy any books. I can always return a shipment and cancel at any time. Even if I never buy another book from Silhouette, the 2 free books and gift are mine to keep forever. So why not take us up on our invitation. You'll be glad you did!

215 SEN CNE7
315 SEN CNE9

Name	(PLEASE PRINT)	
Address	Apt.#	
City	State/Prov.	Zip/Postal Code

* Terms and prices subject to change without notice. Sales tax applicable in N.Y.
** Canadian residents will be charged applicable provincial taxes and GST.
   All orders subject to approval. Offer limited to one per household.
   ® are registered trademarks of Harlequin Enterprises Limited.

SROM99   ©1998 Harlequin Enterprises Limited

Silhouette ROMANCE™

One little...two little...three little...BABIES!

What are three confirmed bachelor brothers to do when they suddenly become guardians to triplets?

Find out in bestselling author
Susan Meier's new trilogy

THE BABY BEQUEST—On sale in January 2000
Evan Brewster needed baby lessons fast! And surprisingly, his father's former assistant seemed to have the perfect knack with the baby brood—and with Evan's heart....

BRINGING UP BABIES—On sale in February 2000
Chas Brewster was desperate to hire a nanny, but what was he to do when he wanted Lily's involvement to become much more personal?

OH, BABIES!—On sale in March 2000
Grant Brewster was known for his control—at least until Kristen sneaked her way into his life. Suddenly the all-so-cool bachelor was getting hot and bothered—and enjoying it!

Available at your favorite retail outlet...only from
SILHOUETTE ROMANCE®

Silhouette®
Where love comes alive™